Praise for Cory Taylor and *Me and Mr Booker*

'One of the best coming-of-age novels I've ever read…
Me and Mr Booker is sexy, smart and brutally funny,
and reminds us that while teenagers grow up fast, it's only
because they're surrounded by adults who behave like children.'
Benjamin Law, author of *The Family Law*

'Restrained, surprisingly moving and compulsively readable,
Cory Taylor's debut novel is a nuanced and touching portrait
of a doomed relationship.' *Sun Herald*

'Cory Taylor's characters are magnificently created.'
Weekend Australian

'One of the most assured debut novels I have ever read.'
Krissy Kneen, author of *Affection*

'Distinctive, disturbing and refreshed by the limitless aptitude
of middle-aged men for acting like spoilt teenagers. A vibrant,
questioning and unpredictable read.' *West Australian*

'★★★★ Sharply observed and blackly comic, but it is also
a tender depiction of love, sex, power and one girl's
heartbreaking step into adulthood.'
Australian Bookseller + Publisher

'Taylor's no-nonsense voice and eagle eye will assure
her of many readers of all ages.' *Age*

'Understated and memorable.' *Canb…*

'An assured debut.' *Sydney Mornin…*

'Controlled and elegant.' David Vann, a…

Cory Taylor is an award-winning screenwriter who has also published short fiction and children's books. She is the Pacific Region Winner of The Commonwealth Book Prize for her first novel, *Me and Mr Booker*. She lives in Brisbane and Japan.

MY BEAUTIFUL ENEMY

CORY TAYLOR

TEXT PUBLISHING MELBOURNE AUSTRALIA

textpublishing.com.au

The Text Publishing Company
Swann House
22 William Street
Melbourne Victoria 3000
Australia

First published in Australia by The Text Publishing Company, 2013

Cover design by W. H. Chong
Page design by Text

Printed and bound in Australia by Griffin Press, an accredited ISO/NZS 1401:2004 Environmental Management System printer

National Library of Australia Cataloguing-in-Publication entry :
Author: Taylor, Cory, 1955-
Title: My beautiful enemy / by Cory Taylor.
ISBN: 9781922079893 (pbk.)
ISBN: 9781921961618 (ebook)
Dewey Number: A823.3

for Shin

Why is the measure of love loss?

Jeanette Winterson

|

Everybody has dreams about the life they might have led. For years I mourned the life I could have shared with Stanley if only the times had been different. I blamed my unhappiness on the war, and then I blamed it on my wives. Now I see that I was unhappy for the same reasons that everyone else, at one time or another, is unhappy. We define ourselves by what we do not have, by the people we are not, and we do this because we must.

When I think back on the man himself, on the real Stanley, as opposed to the imaginary one, I discover that I hardly knew him. I gleaned a little about his early life, and also something about his temperament. But beyond that he was a mystery to me, and therein lay his fascination. In my deluded state back then I imagined I'd found a twin soul. Of course, like a lot of other people, I was blinded by his beauty. In the handful of photographs I've kept of him I can still see it. He stares out of them almost miserably, as if his loveliness is an affliction. Not that I saw it that way, at least not in the beginning. In the beginning I thought it was a kind of miracle.

I met Stanley in the autumn of 1945 at Tatura, a camp for Japanese enemy aliens, where I was stationed as a guard. My first sight of the camp one wet Sunday morning in April had convinced me that my fortunes could sink no lower. It looked like the sleepy place of exile it was: rows and rows of tin and timber army huts arranged in four compounds centring on a parade ground the size of a football pitch, the whole fortress encircled by two fences one inside the other, both topped with rolls of rusted barbed wire. I remember passing through the main gates, my kit slung over my shoulder, and wondering if there hadn't been some terrible mistake. A sheep paddock in the backblocks, a hundred odd miles from Melbourne, was not where I'd planned to take my stand against the enemy. I'd imagined going into battle in some exotic foreign field and mowing down the evil foe before emerging bloodied but triumphant in the dawn light; following my labours there'd be *love and laughter and peace ever after,* if Vera Lynn was to be believed.

I was seventeen years old and still smarting from the comments my instructor had made after my dismissal from the Air Force the previous Christmas. He said I was a good pilot but I lacked character. It was the sort of observation people had been making about me all my life, so I assumed it must be true. Nevertheless the Air Force had been my one chance to redeem myself through acts of true heroism, and the loss of this opportunity had made me bitter to say the least.

I wish I could tell you that things improved after I joined the army, except that the opposite is true. By the time I arrived at Tatura I was so full of self-righteous rage it was laughable. I had hated the army from the start, because it wasn't the Air Force, and because three weeks into my basic training at the Bonegilla barracks, a couple of hours' drive from Tatura, a recurrence of a childhood illness loosely described as 'weak nerves' had relegated me to non-combat tasks with no heroic overtones and not a hint of glamour. I also despised the uniform, which was drab and ill-fitting and didn't flatter anyone who wore it. In my case it made me look green and underfed, like a sickly calf. That this bothered me at all was a measure of my vanity back then. I was the kind of boy who takes everything personally and is over-sensitive to appearances, and Stanley was the same. I believe we had that much in common at least, even if everything else was just a matter of me presuming to know things that were way beyond my comprehension.

Half a lifetime later Stanley would tell me, with a kindly smile, that I imagined he was someone he wasn't. He seemed to be suggesting that I'd misunderstood his actions and exaggerated their significance.

'I never think about the past,' he said in his matinee-idol voice. 'It's over and done with.'

I confessed that for me it was different, and that I dwelled in the past more and more. I told Stanley that for some years now, I'd felt as if my real life had ended when I'd left Tatura, and everything after that had been a posthumous life.

'I remember the whole thing as if it was yesterday,' I said.

'Poor Arthur,' said Stanley and then he took hold of my hand the same way he had when we were boys, lacing his fingers through mine and squeezing so hard it hurt.

Stanley had turned up one night in the middle of May, after I'd been at the camp for little more than a month. I was in the infirmary at the time, suffering the same debilitating headaches and stomach cramps that had made me unfit for active duty. Matron Conlon had confirmed the army doctor's diagnosis. Nerves she said. I needed to learn to relax. To that end she'd installed me in a two-bed ward behind her office where I was to be the sole occupant for as long as it took me to calm down.

Corporal Riley had brought Stanley in after he'd fronted up at the main gate demanding to be let inside. I remember the rain was drumming so hard on the loose tin of the infirmary roof that it was a while before I heard Riley banging on the door. I was the only one awake at the time so I had to let them in through the laundry next to Matron Conlon's office. I'd got into the habit of reading late into the night on a little closed-in section of the back verandah where there was a moth-eaten sofa and chairs and a small library of paperbacks and schoolbooks, whatever came in by way of donations from the Red Cross. It was in the cosy seclusion of this corner that I'd become such a devoted fan of Hemingway's. I believed him when he said that once we have a war there is only one thing to be done. It must be won.

Corporal Riley and Stanley came in out of the storm and waited in the hallway while I went to wake Matron. I remember when we came back Stanley stood to attention and saluted Matron Conlon with a ridiculous flourish, then stared at me with a cool expression as if he'd already decided not to like me. I don't know why this hurt me as much as it did, since I'd only just laid eyes on him and his opinion should have meant nothing to me. I can only think that I was already under his spell.

'Stanley Ueno,' said Matron, chiding him as if this was just the latest in a long string of misdemeanours. When she made no move to introduce me I stepped forward and squared my shoulders.

'Private Arthur Wheeler,' I said.

Without replying, Stanley removed his hat and pushed his damp hair back off his forehead. The first thing you noticed about him was the severity of his features: the eyebrows, nose, full mouth, cheekbones, all cleanly drawn, the overall impression being that his face had been carved with some ideal notion of youth in mind. With his ivory skin and hooded eyes he was by far the handsomest boy I'd ever seen. It almost hurt to look at him, mainly because I would never again be able to take comfort in the common wisdom that the Japs were unlovely. In an instant I'd been converted to a new faith, which said beauty was a rare thing and something to be worshipped unreservedly. I was like a blind man who has suddenly been given the gift of sight, and it struck me that I was in the presence of something wondrous.

'The prodigal son returns,' Riley said to Matron, and then they both stood back and admired him in the manner of proud parents, although the very idea was ludicrous. Matron stood five feet tall and plumply pink all over and Riley had the big-boned heftiness of a carthorse. Stanley, beside them, seemed so princely I had a momentary urge to bow or kneel down before him to show my devotion.

I gathered that Riley and Matron were both glad to see Stanley back, that there'd been some genuine fears for his safety after he'd been reported missing from his Ballarat school. And so I was glad too, without really knowing the reason. At the same time I was still not used to the way Riley and some of the others seemed to regard the Japs as harmless and the camp as a benign institution meant to promote the general welfare of the inmates. I was even baffled by the idea that Jap kids could be let out of the camp to go to school, just as if they were normal kids.

To my way of thinking the Japs were the enemy, before they were individual men, women and children, and that was something never to be forgotten. In those days I was still something of a fanatic and held to the conventional fanatical view that all the local Japanese from places like Broome and Darwin had been locked up out of necessity, as a defence against spy activity and sabotage. I also believed that they weren't strictly human, which was a common enough opinion back then. Either you saw them as superhuman fighting machines, or as primitive beasts, but never as ordinary people.

I felt sorry for Matron Conlon, whose gentleness towards anyone in her care, whether one of us or one of them, had struck me already as foolish.

'They feel the same pain we feel,' she told me. 'We're all God's children.'

I dismissed this view as soon as I heard it because it didn't explain the savagery of the Japanese soldiers I'd read about in the papers, who famously liked to behead their captives with swords or swing enemy babies against the nearest stone wall to crush their skulls. Matron Conlon, I decided, had gone soft in the brain from too much gin; either that or her Irish sentimentality had led her seriously astray.

She motioned for Stanley to come with her into the six-bed ward on the far side of my reading room and I followed, alarmed in case she was planning to let him stay there. By then I'd come to regard the empty infirmary as my private quarters. I remember watching Stanley walk ahead of me, and admiring the way he moved, catlike, with his head held still as if he was on the lookout for prey. Later he told me he'd been so hungry out on the road that he'd tried to hunt and fish. He said if he hadn't been so bad at it he might never have come back to the camp. He might still be out there living in a cave somewhere like a savage. I told him I thought he was better off where he was, fed and clothed and where his family could look out for him, but he turned to me with that cool expression of his and said I had no idea what I was talking about.

'What's he doing here?' I asked Riley, who was sticking close by Stanley and Matron in case there was anything he could do to help.

'Ran away,' said Riley. 'Boarding school not to his liking.'

'What are you talking about?' I said, still confused about Stanley's history.

Riley took hold of my arm and spoke to me in a conspirator's whisper, as if he didn't want Matron to hear.

'I wouldn't hand any child of mine over to the Christian Brothers if my life depended on it. Bunch of kiddie fiddlers.'

His hot breath in my ear made me blush. I worried that Riley might have divined just by looking at me how dim I was about the appetites of men, that he might be offering this as a kind of caution.

In the meantime Matron was examining Stanley under the light, peering at his pupils. She made him open his mouth so she could see his tongue, and then she felt around the base of his ears and under his chin.

Riley let go of my arm and busied himself lighting a fag. He reached out and offered Stanley a puff. We all watched while he put the cigarette to his lips and took a deep drag, his pleasure apparent in the way he closed his eyes and let his head tip back.

'You want me to tell the family you're home?' Riley said. 'Or do you want to surprise them?'

Here it was again, that way of referring to Japs as if they were just like anyone else, acting familiar with them. Stanley didn't say anything. Under the brighter light now I could see how tired he was, how close to collapse, and I had a momentary urge to speak myself, to say something comforting. But since I'd made such a point of keeping my distance from the Japs I couldn't very well change tack now, in front of Riley and Matron, even if my heart had effectively melted inside me.

Matron Conlon stared down at Stanley's wrecked school shoes and made a hissing sound with her tongue.

'Those must be blocks of ice,' she said.

Stanley looked down at his feet and seemed about to swoon.

Riley noticed and, leaping to his side, took hold of the boy's coat sleeve to keep him upright. And then Stanley stared at me again and I blushed more deeply than I had before, because his gaze was so brazen, and because out of my uniform I felt stripped of authority.

That was the other thing about Stanley. It wasn't just his beauty that was so disturbing, but also his refusal to kowtow to anyone. In my first few weeks at the camp, I'd observed for myself how obedient the internees were, almost to the point of servility. But Stanley was different. I discovered later that, although born in Japan, he'd been partly raised by a family in Chicago. I imagined some Chicago public school was where he'd picked up his American swagger and his habit of appearing fearless even when he was quaking in his boots. It was the unflinching face he presented to the world and it fooled most of the people most of the time.

I call him a boy but he wasn't really. He was as solidly built as Riley and bursting out of his school clothes so that the blazer buttonholes gaped.

'Let's get you out of those filthy things,' said Matron Conlon and proceeded to strip Stanley down while Riley helped. I left the ward and watched through the open door from the reading room with my prick stiffening under my dressing-gown. It amuses me now how shocked I was by this development, how horrified that my will to resist my nature had failed me, as it was bound to as soon as I beheld Stanley naked. I was confused enough back then to believe in mind over matter, in the virtue of self-denial. It was only years later that I understood this to be a recipe for despair in all but the most exceptional of men.

Matron Conlon disappeared briefly and came back with a dish of steaming water and a couple of towels. By then Stanley was shivering with the cold. Matron wiped him all over, talking herself through the more tender areas around his buttocks and back where there was a concentration of bruises and scrapes.

'Sure you're lucky those hooligans didn't kill you,' she said. 'I told your mother what would happen to you in that school but of course she had the rest of them saying it'd be for the best.'

Stanley must have been in considerable pain but he didn't complain.

'Well you're the only bloke I know who's tried to break back in here,' said Riley, trying to cheer him up.

'Fetch me the pyjamas there Arthur,' Matron Conlon called out. She indicated the cabinet on the back wall of her office where the laundered pyjamas were stored.

I went to fetch a pair and then sidled back into the bright light where Stanley was standing, one hand covering my stiffy and the other waving the pyjamas at him in a gesture I intended to be imperious. Stanley took them from me and turned away to dress. He hadn't said a word up to that point but now he turned his miraculous head and spoke. He thanked Matron Conlon and asked if he could please go to the toilet and then could he possibly have something to eat because he'd only had stale bread and water since the morning. It was the first time I'd heard his voice. His English was perfect, with an American flatness to it straight out of the movies.

'Where did he learn to talk like that?' I said, once he'd gone to the lavatory. Riley was already out the door in search of food.

'Up and down the highways and byways of America I suppose,' said Matron Conlon, adding that he was lucky he hadn't been shot. It was foolhardy, she said, to show up at the front gate of the camp in the dark without a word to anyone that he was coming.

I found myself yearning for her to let him bunk down where he was, as if my future happiness depended on it. Less than ten minutes ago I'd been concerned he might disrupt my solitude, but now I worried that Matron would decide to send him to the Jap wing of the infirmary to be nursed over there. If that were to happen I wouldn't see him again for days and his absence would be like an extra illness to add to my jangled nerves.

'Which one's his family?' I said.

'Ueno,' said the Matron, as if she expected me to remember names, and when I looked puzzled she listed them. 'Clancy, Frank, Shigeru, Tom, Setsuko, Nancy?'

I drew a blank on all of them.

'My compound?' I said. Each of the four compounds contained about fifty family groups. I was assigned to Compound B where there was a mixed lot of Japs who'd been shipped in at the start of hostilities from places like New Caledonia and Batavia.

'C,' she said. I knew Compound C only by reputation. The men said it was the best-run compound in the camp, because the Japs there were trusted to keep things reasonable. Trouble in Compound C was apparently dealt with internally whereas trouble in the other compounds had a tendency to spill over. So far there had been no serious trouble in the entire camp as far as I could tell. The internees seemed content to be well fed and out of harm's way. This pretty much described the guards too. They may as well have been in charge of a herd of fat cows, the way they conducted themselves. It was dispiriting, in that it was just what I'd come to expect of the army, laziness combined with low-level venality. It injured my vanity to be associated with the whole unedifying business.

'He's big for a Jap,' I said.

'He is that,' said Matron in a dreamy way, because of the drink and because she was still half-asleep. 'I haven't met the father, but the uncle's a big strapping man.'

'Where's the father?' I said.

'He was visiting his parents in Japan when they bombed Pearl Harbor and nobody's heard a thing from him since that day.'

'What were they doing in America?' I said.

'They're a travelling circus,' said Matron. 'So I suspect they were travelling.'

And then she said I should stop hanging around here chattering. 'You're missing out on your beauty sleep,' she said.

I refused to move. Riley eventually returned with a packet of biscuits and a can of Carnation milk, which he decided to heat up on the burner in Matron's office.

'Where's he going to sleep?' I said, hoping to catch another glimpse of Stanley before he turned in.

'I'll let him stay over this side,' she said, 'where you can keep an eye on him. Since you've nothing better to do with your time.'

And that is how it all started, the period of my life I call The War, even if this is only a reference to my own personal victories and losses at the time and not to the larger catastrophe that produced them. As I tried to explain to Stanley, when we were both men on the verge of middle age, it wasn't the historical events that continued to haunt me; it was the private world in which his life and mine had collided so painfully. That was a wound, I said, that refused to heal over.

2

I'd tried to warn May about my poor character when we first met.

'I'm bad news,' I told her.

'What's that supposed to mean?' she said.

I told her I'd been pronounced a juvenile delinquent at twelve and parcelled out to foster homes, which was a lie, and I said I'd run away from school to join the Air Force, which was the truth.

'I should be blowing up Germany right now,' I told her, 'but they decided to keep me in reserve in case General MacArthur calls.'

This was in January 1945, just after I'd joined the army. Less than a fortnight into basic training I'd snuck out of the Bonegilla barracks on a Saturday night to go to a dance in the town. May had spotted me across a crowded room. I looked like Errol Flynn on his night off, she used to tell me, and from the first moment

I spoke, she said, there was only me in the hall and her, as if everyone else had just dropped through a hole in the floor.

And I would tell her—because it was true—that she was the first girl I'd ever met who didn't giggle and act shy whenever I looked sideways at her. On the contrary she'd stared me down with a solemn concentration I found very appealing. It had singled her out as the serious one in her group. I'd already decided that her friends were all spoilt private school girls slumming it in the Land Army. The ringleader Katherine had kept patting me on the knee and telling me I looked like a puppy she'd left at home in Toorak. May, on the other hand, had remained very quiet, looking sideways at me with an expression of something close to rapture.

'I was drunk,' she said. 'Katherine had brought along some cooking sherry and we polished it off in the car before we even got there.'

I remember while we were dancing she told me with some passion that I was bloody lucky just to be alive. She was leaning into my shoulder by then so I could see right down the front of her dress to where her breasts were squeezed together like two big melons in a sack.

'You should bloody well count your blessings,' she said. She smelled powdery, like my mother Doris, and she was pink and freckly like Doris too, in a way that made me instantly homesick.

'What shall I call you?' I said, on the way to getting drunk myself.

'You can call me Miss Forbes,' she said, grinning.

Once we were back at our table I asked her about her family

and she told me her father was in building and that she was the youngest of three.

'Ian's the eldest,' she said. 'He's in an essential service so he doesn't have to join up.'

'What essential service?' said Katherine.

'Trucking,' she said.

Katherine burst out laughing and then apologised. 'I thought you said something else,' she said, placing her hand over her mouth to control her giggles.

May reached over to slap Katherine on the wrist and then stared at me again.

'My middle brother Owen is in a Jap POW camp somewhere,' she said. 'But we don't actually know if he's alive or dead.'

'I'm sorry,' I said.

'So am I,' she said, her grey eyes brimming with tears. 'I miss him all the time.'

After that I saw her every few weeks on my day off because she was living in the town of Bonegilla in a boarding house and it was a good excuse to get away from the life of a soldier for a few hours. Also because she was easy to be with, very warm and what my mother would have called *natural*. She thought nothing, for instance, of kissing me on the mouth on my second visit to her room, or of placing my hand on her breast the next time I was there. When I took it off she was disappointed.

I apologised.

'Don't,' she said. 'It's not your fault. It's just that I feel like I can trust you.'

I couldn't think of what to say to her so I put my hand back on her breast and kissed her again and I kept doing that for a few minutes until she asked me to stop because Katherine might come back from her shower at any moment.

She got up to turn the radio on and make us some more tea on the little burner the girls had rigged up in the corner of their room.

'Why did you join the AIF?' she said once she was settled back on the bed next to me.

'Because I was too good-looking for the Air Force,' I said.

She smiled and I noticed the way it made dimples in the middle of her cheeks.

'Did they chuck you out because of some girl?'

I decided to tell her the truth, or most of it.

'I went on a bender with Nigel Rutherford after my first solo flight and broke my ankle falling off a stolen motor bike, so I missed out on graduating.'

'Who's Nigel Rutherford?' she said.

'A bloke I knew back then,' I said. 'A navigator. He's in England now, right in the thick of things.'

Her smile faded and she regarded me with her usual solemnity.

'Does it worry you,' she said, 'the idea of fighting?'

I wasn't prepared for this. It was a fair enough question but so unexpected that I almost laughed.

'I didn't crash the bike deliberately,' I said. 'If that's what you mean.'

May watched me over the rim of her cup as she sipped her tea.

'It's just that you seem so nervous all the time,' she said.

'It's like you're afraid someone's going to blame you.'

'Blame me for what?' I said. I was trembling by then, and my cheeks were on fire.

'Whatever it is you're hiding,' she said in a hushed voice, as if we were plotters in some conspiracy.

I can't explain the bond that formed between me and May at that moment but I think I felt it more intensely because I was so friendless at the time, and because mention of Nigel and my time in the Air Force had only served to remind me how lonely and miserable I was in the army. It seemed the most punishing way a person could live, being marched up and down all day in the blazing sun and lectured on a dozen different ways to kill a man and make him stay dead. If I thought about actual warfare and what it would be like to put all this theory into practice, I realised why I'd always preferred the idea of bombing the enemy from a great height to the idea of meeting him face to face and stabbing him in his warm guts with my bayonet.

'Are you calling me a coward?' I said.

'I couldn't care less if you are or not,' she said. 'I just don't want to lose you.'

It was the kindest thing anyone had said to me in months and, to my eternal shame, I burst into tears and sat slumped against the wall snivelling and whining and feeling unbearably sorry for myself. May hugged me and stroked my hair and told me how she thought if I was killed in the war or taken prisoner she would feel like her life was over too. And that was when she told me she loved me and I kissed her properly for the first time, without feeling at all self-conscious or shy.

Of course I regret now that I didn't put a stop to things immediately; that way I could have saved us both a lot of pain. My only excuse is that back then I was too ignorant to think any harm could come from simply following the girl's lead and giving her what she seemed to want, even if my own desires went largely unanswered. Moreover, the way I saw it I owed May for having rescued me right at the point when I thought the army might be doing me irreparable damage. It helped that she was nineteen, two years older than me, and also that she was the motherly type.

Katherine had already warned me about what was going to happen next.

'She's always picking up waifs and strays,' she said. 'She takes them home and fattens them up and in a few weeks they're unrecognisable.'

'Do I look worried?' I said.

'Not worried enough,' said Katherine. She didn't like me very much. According to May, Katherine had decided I had tickets on myself.

When May told me this I laughed because it was exactly the same thing my father had always said about me.

'I was an arrogant little upstart,' I said, mimicking my father's fury at something I'd done or not done, 'who didn't know his place, and I was either in for a very rude awakening indeed, or I was going to get my comeuppance.'

'Poor Arthur,' said May.

I told her not to feel sorry for me.

'He actually did me a favour,' I said. 'He showed me what I was up against. It doesn't always follow that parents love their children, or that husbands love their wives, because sometimes they don't. Sometimes love has nothing to do with it.'

May didn't believe me. She shook her head to indicate that I didn't know what I was talking about.

'My family is everything to me,' she said. 'And I know they're going to love you.'

'I hope so,' I said.

And I did, for my sake more than for May's, because if they didn't, and she was forced to choose between her family and me, she might abandon me as suddenly as she'd saved me.

There is no joy for me in recalling any of these feelings now because they were of no real help to me once Stanley showed up in the middle of the night dripping wet from the rain. After that I was lost, my lack of character confirmed, all of my good intentions regarding May and her loving family abandoned in favour of my new fascination for a Jap boy I'd only just clapped eyes on. And worse was to come, because I reasoned that this needn't matter, that nobody need know about my change of heart, since self-preservation dictated I keep it a secret—a philosophy I've stuck by ever since. It was as if my father's dark predictions had all come true, though not in the way he'd envisaged. My long-awaited comeuppance had arrived. I was tempted to telephone home to let my father know how a Jap runaway had helped me see the light, and I would have, if I hadn't made a vow some months before to never, ever speak to him again.

3

The day after the storm Stanley slept, and the day after that. Matron Conlon had prescribed him bed rest and three square meals a day, and he behaved like a model patient. I, on the other hand, was a terrible disappointment to her since I still couldn't keep my food down properly. Every time I ate something my stomach heaved and my headaches returned so I was placed on a child's diet of pureed vegetables and warm milk. Nevertheless, I managed to keep an eye on Stanley just as Matron Conlon had asked me to, hanging in the doorway of the reading room so I had a clear view of his bed. Occasionally I would replenish his water or help him to the toilet. Then I'd sit in the chair beside him and watch him drift back to sleep again. It was as though the effort to keep his eyes open for any longer than a few minutes was too much for him. He would do his best, even trying to make small talk, but then the lids would lower over his brown eyes and he would be dead to the world.

I knew when he was dreaming: I would look up from my book and he would be murmuring something under his breath, his facial expressions turning frightened and comically sombre in turns. Sometimes it was hard to know whether he was asleep or awake during these dreams because his eyes would open halfway and he would say things that almost made sense. *I'm not a Jap*, he said once, which struck me as funny. Once he cried real tears in his sleep and called out someone's name. I only knew it was a name because it ended with *san*, and I'd learned by then to recognise that word along with a few others some kids had taught me.

I say his eyes were brown, but actually they were golden. With the sun shining directly into them they glowed like pools of honey and you could see the tiny flecks of green in them that seemed to have no business being there. Most Japs had dark eyes all identically shaped, I thought, so that I still found it hard to tell them apart or to read their emotions with any confidence. They didn't like to look at you anyway.

I'd noticed this with the kids who'd been to Japan for their schooling, as a lot of them had, especially the boys. Out of all the kids in the camp, numbering around two hundred, there were forty or so who'd been sent home to family members back in Japan at some point in their lives. For this reason they had different manners and gestures from the rest of them. They would refuse to see you, even though you could be talking right at them. I assumed this was something they'd been taught, although now I wonder if a lot of them weren't merely shy. At the time, however, it struck me as impolite and I made it my business to tell them to meet my gaze and answer me clearly whenever I asked a question. I still thought it was my business to reform them. I believed that they were in need of instruction in the superior culture of men like me, who'd had the great good fortune to be born British subjects.

My youth and arrogance back then ensured that I lived by this ridiculous creed even after the British Empire had expired so spectacularly. It was many years before I realised the significance of Singapore's fall, and many more years before I came to understand how fatuous my basic assumptions about the world had been up until that point. We'd all been lied to of course, the Japs included. They'd believed in their lies and we'd believed in ours. Stanley was the only person I'd ever met who appeared to believe in nothing at all but his own talent for survival.

I quizzed Matron Conlon relentlessly, firing questions about Stanley at her every time she came to check on him.

'Did he go to school in America?' I said.

'I expect so,' said Matron Conlon.

I showed her the contents of his suitcase. He'd carried at least thirty books back from Ballarat as well as letters and souvenirs from abroad.

'Is the family pleased he's come back?' I said.

'What do you think?' said Matron Conlon. 'It was them who moved heaven and earth to get him out of here. Wrote back and forth to the government for months. Got the camp commandant to plead their case.'

'Why?' I said.

'Because all of the kiddies are wasting their days here when they should be getting proper schooling,' she said. 'You've seen that for yourself.'

It hadn't occurred to me that this was what the kids were doing until Matron pointed it out to me. Even so I couldn't muster a great deal of sympathy for them. I took it for granted that the point of being an enemy alien was that you be deprived of all the rights of ordinary citizens.

'Are they all circus people?' I said. I'd seen the circus posters in Stanley's suitcase, as well as a scrapbook full of newspaper cuttings, some with photographs in them featuring Stanley as a small boy smiling out of a row of performers.

'All the men,' she said. 'Not his mother. She was a farm girl, an arranged match I gather.'

'Is Stanley his real name?' I said. 'Or just a stage name.'

Matron Conlon said she had no idea but if I was so interested why didn't I ask Stanley myself.

'See what you can weasel out of him,' she said. 'I suspect there's a great deal going on in that lovely head of his, and it'll do you good to listen to someone else's troubles for a change instead of dwelling on your own.'

'You think I don't know that?' I said, gazing at Stanley and willing him to wake up.

It wasn't until the third day that I managed to have a proper conversation with him. By then the sun had finally returned after more than a week of foul weather. When I came to his doorway in the morning he was sitting up in bed eating a boiled egg with some bread and butter and sipping steaming tea out of a tin mug. The winter sun streamed into the room from the high windows beside him so that his face was sliced in half, one side blindingly white and the other side a black silhouette. As he raised his mug to take another sip of tea the steam billowed up through the light and made half a halo around the sunlit side of his head. I'd seen a similar effect in the cinema, done with artificial lights and cigarette smoke and I had a momentary vision of Stanley as a handsome villain in some spy thriller set in the perfumed Far East.

'Morning,' I said.

I spoke to him from the doorway. I told him my name in case he'd forgotten it and informed him that I was normally a guard.

'Stanley Ueno,' he replied. 'I'm normally an acrobat.'

He was mocking me, or flirting with me, I wasn't sure which. Either way it was a sign that he intended to treat me with absolutely no deference. I didn't know whether I should be angry or flattered so for a moment I just stared at him and said nothing.

'What's wrong with you?' he said.

I told him I couldn't eat anything.

'Bad luck,' he said. 'The food here's so good. Not like over in the mess.'

I said I didn't think there was any difference.

'The major difference,' he said, 'is that you can eat it in bed without hundreds of other people all shovelling it in at the same time like pigs at a trough. This is so thoroughly civilised.' He gestured around at the room, at his books, now unpacked, piled up on the bedside table, at his neat covers and his plump pillows. 'The only thing missing is a cigarette and a paper so I can see how the New York Yankees are faring.'

'Would you like me to ring down to reception?' I said.

'Please be so kind,' he said, smiling at his own joke.

I noticed how square and straight his teeth were. So many of the other kids had gaps where their rotten teeth had been pulled. I must have been staring because Stanley asked me if there was something on his face.

'No,' I said. 'You're perfect.'

That made him laugh. 'Why thank you,' he said, fluttering his eyelids and pretending to be embarrassed.

'I saw you when you first came in.'

'I don't remember.'

'You were in pretty bad shape.' I said.

'I'm improving by the minute,' he said, 'thanks to your excellent care and attention.'

'All part of the service,' I said.

It was unheard of to be talking to a Jap in this way, both of us in our pyjamas, him lying in his bed. I leaned on the doorframe, hesitant to come any closer in case he saw how nervous I was. I couldn't stop trembling. He, on the other hand, seemed perfectly relaxed. Two days of solid meals and uninterrupted sleep had transformed him, made his skin clear and his eyes bright.

'What happened to you out there?' I said.

'You ask a lot of questions.'

'Matron Conlon told me to press you for information.'

'Do you always do as you're told?'

'First thing they teach you in the army.'

'I wouldn't know,' he said, his mood shifting. He had a way of clamming up suddenly, whenever a conversation turned in a direction he didn't care for, and it never seemed wise to probe too deeply, not if you wanted to keep him as a friend. At the same time he could be forthright about things that he wanted you to know and this was how he kept you constantly off balance. It was like he had two different personalities, one cold and critical and the other passionate and temperamental.

'I don't suppose you play cards?' I said. It was something to fill the lull in the conversation. I showed him the pack of cards I'd put in the pocket of my dressing-gown, on the off chance that he might agree to a game of poker.

'Maybe later,' he said. 'I need a bath first.'

'Do you want any help?' I said, my pulse quickening at the thought of helping him to undress.

'I think I can manage,' he said.

I gestured to the table and chairs that were set up in the corridor for socialising.

'Meet you when you're ready,' I said.

He nodded and smiled again and then regarded me with something like sadness, as if he already felt sorry for me for some private reason of his own.

'I hope you like losing,' he said.

'I've had a lot of practice,' I said, smiling back at him.

He raised his hand and waved goodbye in a gesture that was almost dismissive. For a boy of fifteen he seemed to have an enormous reserve of scorn for people like me, people who, in his estimation I'm sure, had yet to suffer.

I went back to the ward and waited for what I judged was enough time for him to finish in the bath. My thoughts turned inevitably to May. I knew exactly what she would make of my courting Stanley in this way. She would see it as a betrayal, which is exactly what it was. In my own defence I reasoned that I was only taking advantage of the opportunity to figure out what made the Japs tick. I told myself I had a duty to get to know my enemy. After all, when Stanley and I were both well again, we would simply go back to our respective lives and have nothing to do with one another. Of course this took no account of my true feelings, which were in a state of unholy turmoil, or of my real intention, which was to put myself in Stanley's way as often as circumstance allowed.

When I returned to the corridor I found him seated at the card table shuffling the pack I'd left there, using various tricks he must have picked up from years of hanging around card sharps. He was showing off for Matron Conlon. She stood beside him with her hands on her stocky hips, gawping with admiration.

'Sure did you ever see anyone as deft as that?' she said when I was standing beside her. 'He's like a piece of oiled machinery.' You could tell when she'd been drinking because she smelled of the cough lollies she sucked on to mask the gin.

Stanley fanned the pack out with his right hand then swiftly flipped all fifty-two cards on their faces with a single movement of his left.

'Pick a card,' he told Matron Conlon.

She reached out and took a card.

'Don't show it to me,' he said.

She hid the card against her bosom.

He gathered the cards up again, cut the pack, then told

Matron Conlon to place her chosen card on the top of one of the piles.

'Either will do,' he said.

When she'd done as she was told he shuffled the cards again so fast his hands were a blur, at the same time throwing one single card a foot in the air. It landed face up on the table, the six of spades.

'That's not possible,' said Matron Conlon. 'How in the Lord's name did you do that?'

Stanley grinned first at her and then at me, and I saw again the flecks of green in his eyes where the sun was making them glow. With his face freshly scrubbed and his raven hair combed back he resembled some sleek creature just surfaced out of the sea.

'Tricks of the trade,' he said.

Matron shook her head in disbelief. 'You be careful,' she said to me. 'Are you sure you know what you're getting yourself into?'

'I have no idea,' I said.

She told us to keep our voices down in case some nosey parker decided to come poking around where he didn't belong. Strictly speaking, she said, we were not supposed to be fraternising.

'I'll keep a weather eye out,' I said.

'I won't take the blame,' she said, 'if you're found out.'

She stared at us, trying to seem stern, but the truth was she had no time for the rules and regulations. She ran the infirmary her way, like it was home and the patients were family. And she was at ease with secrets, having so many of her own. The truth is I would have liked to stay curled up under her fleshy, inebriated wing for the rest of the war. The prospect of putting on my uniform again and returning to guard duties once my nerves settled down filled me with dread. I gave Matron Conlon a lazy salute and watched her bustle away. You could hear her stockings brushing against each other as her thick legs met and separated again. It was like she was walking through a field of corn.

4

The next two days were the happiest I ever spent with Stanley.
While Matron Conlon tended his cuts and bruises and the orderly
fetched him gargantuan meals, I stayed close by like a sidekick,
someone to amuse him and distract him from his real worries. I
wasn't sure precisely what these were because he never told me,
but I had the sense that in the eyes of his family he'd made a
mistake by coming back to the camp when they'd gone to so
much trouble to get him out. I only knew this because I was there
when his uncle Shigeru came to visit him, trailed by his pale and
silent mother.

I didn't recognise either of them and they didn't introduce
themselves. Shigeru simply stood very tall and straight beside
Stanley's bed and stared at me through his glasses, while Mrs
Ueno bowed her head repeatedly in my direction. She was a

strange sight to behold, with her unravelling garments and her fierce glower. When I failed to budge from my chair Shigeru removed his crumpled felt hat, revealing a shock of hair that sprang straight up off his forehead like a rooster's comb.

'This is a private business,' he said, smiling at me mirthlessly. 'If you will please excuse yourself.'

Stanley's mother stopped bowing and grabbed hold of Shigeru's jacket as if to steady him. She looked at me so imploringly I was forced to stand up and leave the room.

Later I asked Stanley what all the subsequent yelling had been about. Even though some of it had been in English I hadn't caught the thrust of the argument.

'Nothing,' he said.

'Didn't sound like nothing to me,' I said.

He did an impromptu impersonation of his uncle berating him, calling him names, telling him what a failure he was: 'It's a good thing your father's not here. He'd be ashamed to have you as his son,' he yelled, in a high-pitched squeal that was a perfect rendition of his uncle's rage.

'Did you tell him you were beaten up at school?' I said.

'Who said I was beaten up at school?' said Stanley.

'I just assumed,' I said.

He paused then fell on the sofa as if he'd been shot.

'I deserved it,' he said. 'I was lucky they didn't kill me.'

I asked him who 'they' were but he waved a hand in front of his face to indicate it wasn't worth pursuing the topic. And then he rolled onto his side and propped his head up on one arm so his gaze was level with mine.

'Do you know anything about baseball?' he said.

'Sorry,' I said. 'Tennis is my game.'

This made him collapse onto his back again and hoot with laughter. He repeated what I'd just said, mimicking the way I spoke with cruel accuracy.

'Fuck off,' I said.

'Tennis doesn't count,' he said. 'It's like comparing a game of chess with a game of checkers.'

'Do you even play tennis?' I said.

'I play everything,' he said. 'Apart from water sports. I don't like getting naked unless it's for money.'

If he noticed me blushing he didn't let on. I proceeded to tell him how tennis was a game where mental strength was more important than physical strength.

'Who told you that load of horseshit?' he said.

'My tennis teacher,' I said. 'Ex-junior state champion. Bill Humphries was his name. He used to live next door to me when I was growing up.'

'How come he didn't make the senior team?' said Stanley.

I didn't reply. Stanley looked at me and broke into a sympathetic smile, as if he'd decided to feel sorry for me.

'You want to know why I came back here?' he said.

'I couldn't care less,' I said.

'Because nobody in Ballarat knows the difference between a curveball and a slider is why. I never met a more ignorant bunch of queers in my entire life.'

The earnest way he said it made me laugh.

'You think I'm joking?' he said.

'Exaggerating,' I said.

'Yeah well that's probably because you're one of them,' he said, climbing off the sofa and dancing around the room with an invisible tennis racket calling out the score in a woman's falsetto. *Fifteen-love thirty-love forty-love game. Jolly good show chaps.*

'Why didn't you just disappear somewhere?' I said. 'You could have gone anywhere you wanted.'

He came over to where I was sitting and leaned over to rest his hands on the arms of the chair so he could stare right at me from a foot away.

'Look at my face,' he said. 'What do you see?'

I was too afraid to tell him. The truth was I couldn't see anything because my eyes had suddenly refused to focus. But I could feel his warm breath on my face and smell the laundered cotton of his pyjamas, and I could also feel myself going hard so I pulled the flaps of my dressing-gown shut as if I was chilly.

'Jap,' he said. 'That's what you see.'

'Is that why you were beaten up?' I said, hoping he would stand and move away so I could breathe normally again. But he stayed where he was.

'What do you think?' he said.

'I'm sorry,' I said.

'No you're not,' he said, finally straightening up. He stretched his back with a grimace, a sign that his injuries were still causing him pain.

'You're nothing like a Jap,' I said, blurting it out before I'd even begun to comprehend the naivety of thinking that his Yank swagger was the true Stanley. Hadn't he just told me that his face alone was the thing that defined him in the eyes of the world?

Stanley glared down at me and shook his head. And then he did something that I have trouble believing even now, given the fact that Matron Conlon was in her office next door having her morning tea. He leaned over again and kissed me on the cheek.

'I bet you're sorry now,' he said.

I don't remember if I replied. I think I just sat there and watched him walk towards the doorway.

'Nature calls,' he said as he left the room.

When he came back I was still sitting in the chair exactly where he'd left me. I waited for him to return to the sofa and get settled.

'You shouldn't have done that,' I said.

Stanley ignored me and gazed out of the window at the boundary fence that ran along the back of the infirmary. Beyond that there was a field where sheep grazed and the occasional family of wallabies stopped to feed on the patchy grass.

'I promise I won't do it again,' he said, without taking his eyes off the scene outside.

And then I told Stanley that he wasn't the first boy who'd ever kissed me. I told him how Nigel Rutherford had kissed me on the back of the neck while we were riding a stolen motor bike and had nearly killed the both of us. I pulled up the leg of my pyjama pants to show him my scars.

'Nasty,' he said.

'You should have seen Nigel,' I said. 'They had to scrape him off the road.'

'Serves him right,' said Stanley. 'Bloody pervert.'

I laughed so much that Matron Conlon came to the door and asked what the joke was. She'd brought us both a cup of tea and I leaped up to take the tray from her, terrified in case she'd overheard our conversation.

'Arthur's just telling me the story of his tragic love life,' said Stanley.

Matron Conlon looked at Stanley then at me, then at Stanley again, then she gave us one of her smiles, the kind you give to children who are misbehaving. She was already red in the face from her morning tipple.

'Sure isn't he in the business of breaking hearts,' she said, staring pointedly in my direction. She knew about May because I'd told her, even venturing to confess that I might actually be in love.

'Legs actually,' I said, trying to act the clown.

Stanley started giggling so hard he had to hold his hands to his bruised ribs.

'Are you all right there?' said Matron Conlon. 'Do you want me to strap you up?'

Stanley shook his head.

Matron turned to me and adopted what she must have considered to be her sternest expression.

'You need to take a leaf out of Stanley's book,' she said.

'Which one?' I said. 'He has so many.'

She wagged a finger at me. 'You'll never get your strength back if you don't make the effort to eat,' she said. 'You're not getting the nourishment you need to put some meat on those bones, the way Stanley here is doing. Sure you'll fade away to nothing.'

Stanley rolled up his sleeve and raised his right arm, bending it and clenching his fist in a strongman display. He beckoned for me to come over and feel how hard his biceps were. I put down the tea tray and did as I was told, while Matron Conlon watched.

'What's your secret?' I said.

'Mental strength,' said Stanley, mocking me again.

If Matron Conlon hadn't been there I would have slapped him.

After she left Stanley said he wanted to go back to bed and sleep for a while. He also said, as if it was an order, that I should come with him because it was warmer in his ward than in the reading room. So I went and sat in the bedside chair and tried to concentrate on my book. I remember I'd discovered a collection of essays by George Orwell on the bookshelves and had started to read *Shooting an Elephant*. At the point where he says that the whites in Burma were frequently spat upon, I put the book down and watched the sheep moving in single file across the sunlit field outside the fence. It occurred to me at that moment that I was probably the object of a similar loathing myself among the Japs. Just because I'd never been spat at in the camp didn't mean there weren't people there who despised me. It was even possible that Stanley was only pretending to be my friend because he had no other alternative. But then I remembered his kiss. It had been too reckless to suggest any kind of a pretext. I could still feel the spot on my cheek where his lips had touched my skin. It seemed to give off a special heat like a burn or a cut.

It was ridiculous what I did next. Moved by something like a child's longing to be picked up and held, I crossed the room and closed the door into the reading room. Then I jammed my chair in under the doorhandle and, after I was satisfied that I was safe against unexpected interruptions, I went over to Stanley's bed and lay down next to him. He was so deeply asleep that he didn't stir, even when I put my arm around his waist and drew myself in towards his back. I say it was ridiculous, but it was also intoxicating, like being both drunk and abnormally alert at the same time. I stayed there for twenty minutes, long enough to feel the heat of Stanley's body transfer itself to me and close enough to commit to memory how the whorl of his ear ended in a lobe shaped like a pea.

Of course now I wonder if he wasn't awake the whole time and only pretending to be asleep, and whether that somehow explains why his mood was noticeably worse later on that same day. I'd eaten my meal, such as it was, in the small infirmary canteen, where Matron could watch over me. When I came back along the verandah to the reading room I found Stanley sitting on the sofa with his nose in a book. He was eating at the same time, distractedly shovelling in great spoonfuls of shepherd's pie and carrots. I stood over him and watched.

'You want some?' he said.

I told him I'd already had my dinner.

'What did you have?' he said.

'Custard,' I said. 'And something stewed.'

'I can't stand custard,' he said. 'It's like eating snot.'

He seemed broody and upset.

'What's the matter?' I said.

He was silent. He finished eating and laid his dinner tray on the arm of the sofa, wiping his mouth on his sleeve as he did so.

'Did you ever want to kill anyone?' he said.

'My father,' I answered straightaway.

'Why him?' said Stanley.

'He liked to torment me,' I said. 'Punish me for no reason. He'd lock me up in a cupboard and leave me there for hours. So I used to sit in the dark and plot how I was going to murder him and make it look like an accident.'

'Where are you from?' he asked.

'The country,' I said. 'What about you?'

'Kyushu,' he said.

I took down a well-thumbed encyclopaedia that was sitting on the library shelves among the children's books and opened it at a map of the world. Stanley pointed to a spot near Nagasaki on the green map of Japan and I pointed to a spot in the far north of New South Wales where the country was coloured empire pink.

'There's nothing there,' I said. 'It's a shithole.'

Then Stanley told me he'd tried to kill one of the boys at his boarding school by pushing him down some stairs. 'It wasn't a plan or anything,' he said. 'He was just there and nobody was watching.'

He paused and ran his hand through his hair to push it back off his forehead. He suddenly seemed very old, as if what he was telling me had happened decades ago, when it had really only been a matter of days.

'The headmaster called me in to his office the next morning,' he said, 'and I told him the boy had been running and had tripped over his own feet.'

'Did he believe you?' I said.

'After I sucked his dick,' he said.

I looked away, but Stanley had already witnessed my embarrassment and was laughing at me. I think he was pleased that he'd managed to shock me so easily.

'You want me to show you how?'

'No,' I said. 'Don't be disgusting.'

Later, while we were playing a game of Chinese checkers, he told me that he'd also tried to kill one of his teachers, but when I asked why he just got up and walked out of the room. I waited a few minutes before following him. I found him around the back of the lavatory smoking a cigarette that he must have begged or stolen from over at the Jap ward while I was sleeping. He was crying. He didn't try to hide it. He let the tears roll down his cheeks and drip onto the front of his dressing-gown.

'What's the trouble?' I said.

He looked away from me and leaked smoke out of his nose and mouth. Before I could stop myself I'd reached over and touched his sleeve, intending to comfort him, but it was as if I'd struck him. He pulled his arm away violently without turning around, so I just stood there and didn't say another word until he told me to leave.

'I don't want to,' I said. 'And there's no need to talk to me as if I'm an imbecile.'

'Actually there's no need to talk to you at all,' he said.

I didn't reply. I decided it was none of my business anyway, what he'd done or hadn't done. I even suspected that he'd simply made up a story to impress me. I'd lied myself, many times, so I knew how easy it was to get into the habit. I went off to bed and spent a restless night slipping in and out of a complicated dream about May, in which she wanted to know why I'd shot my father dead when he hadn't done anything to deserve such harsh treatment. I kept on telling her that people like my father were better off dead but she'd refused to listen and in the end I'd agreed to go to the Burmese police to explain my special circumstances and to beg for mercy.

The next day it was as if Stanley had forgotten the whole episode. I found him sitting up in bed, eating his boiled eggs and toast, smiling at some private joke.

'You look terrible,' he said, while I hovered in the doorway waiting to be invited in.

'I didn't sleep too well,' I said.

'I slept like a baby,' he said, and then he told me he'd asked Matron Conlon for a discharge. 'I don't see the point of staying in bed any longer when I feel perfectly fine.'

'What did she say?' I asked, dreading the answer.

'I'm going tomorrow.'

'Going where? Are they sending you back to school?'

'They can try. Would you miss me?'

'Not fucking likely,' I said.

I crossed the room to pick up my Orwell book off his bedside table where I'd left it the previous afternoon.

'What are you reading?' he said.

I sat down next to him on the bedcovers and showed him.

'What's it about?' he said.

'I'll tell you when I've finished.'

'What's your guess?'

'The dirty work of empire,' I said, pointing out the phrase that had unsettled me the most when I'd come across it the day before.

'Would I like it?' he said.

'Depends what kind of stuff you read,' I said.

I took down one of his books from the windowsill where he'd piled them up. I stared at the cover illustration and the Japanese characters that spelled out the title.

'That's Akutagawa,' he said. 'He's pretty good, but I generally prefer American writers to Japanese writers.'

'Why?'

'Because Americans think big and Japanese think small.'

'And that's why they're trying to take over the entire world?' I said.

He smiled at me showing off his square front teeth.

'They're going to lose,' he said.

'You mean the Japs?' I said, 'or the Yanks?'

He looked at me as if I was mentally deficient. 'America is the richest country in the world,' he said. 'You should see the cars they drive around in and the houses they live in and the amount of food they eat.'

'Did you like it there?'

'I'm sorry I ever left,' he said, staring at the book by Akutagawa in my lap. I gave it back to him and he returned it to the pile on the windowsill.

'Why did you?' I said.

'We go where there's work,' he said. 'And my father thought we'd be safer here if there was a war.'

'Bad mistake,' I said, and regretted it as soon as I saw the scorn on Stanley's face. 'I only mean it wouldn't have made much difference in the end,' I continued, trying to sound philosophical on his behalf. 'You'd have been interned in America anyway.'

'You don't say,' he said.

We were silent for a minute or so and then I said that I'd dreamed of going to America ever since I was a kid.

'Is it the same as it looks in the movies?'

'Better,' he said. 'It's the best place on earth if you've got any kind of ambition or talent.'

'That's what Bill used to tell me,' I said. 'He said I could make a living on the professional tennis circuit there if I was good enough.'

Stanley looked out the window and shook his head slowly as if I was a lost cause.

'There's only one game in America,' said Stanley. 'I told you that already.'

'Then maybe I'll switch,' I said, desperate to win his approval. It was worse than hunger, this longing I had for him to like me.

'The point is I'm not hanging around here once the war's over,' I said. 'Much better to be someplace where there's real opportunity.'

Stanley wasn't listening. He was gazing out at the paddock on the other side of the fence, where at least a hundred white cockatoos had wheeled in low. They were like a huge flying carpet that had settled just above the ground but kept fluttering and lifting at the corners. You could hear them chattering, trying to decide if it was safe to land.

'I'm going to join up,' he said.

I stared at him and didn't know what to say.

'There are plenty of Japs in the AIF,' he said. 'Interpreters, intelligence officers, spies.'

I told him I didn't think he had a hope in hell of getting a job like that.

'Why not?' he said, turning to look at me. 'I've already tried to kill two people. They could use someone like me.'

'You're an alien,' I said. 'You don't qualify.'

'I'll forge my papers,' he said.

I couldn't tell if he was joking or not so I refrained from smiling.

And that's when Stanley took hold of my hand and laced his fingers through mine, squeezing so hard it felt like my bones were about to snap. I think he meant it as a warning, to show how much violence there was in him, but it didn't scare me. If anything I enjoyed the pain. When he finally tried to let go I resisted and then he wrestled my arm nearly out of its socket. I fought back, grabbing hold of him with my free arm and dragging him off his bed. For ten minutes we grappled with each other in a contest of wills, without holding back, but without trying to injure each other either, just tussling and flailing blindly around in circles until we both fell exhausted to the floor.

'I won,' said Stanley.

'Bullshit,' I said.

'You want to go again one day when we get out of here?'

It was more of a threat than an invitation.

'You're on,' I said.

I scrambled to get up because I didn't want Stanley to see how close to tears I was. He had in fact won the fight, but that wasn't the reason I wanted to cry. It was more that I was so uncertain of where I stood with him. One minute he was making jokes with me about Nigel Rutherford and the next minute he was trying to break my hand. And now he'd asked to be sent back to his compound early, when all I wanted was for the two of us to stay in the infirmary for as long as we could, reading and playing cards like two schoolboys on a permanent holiday. It was so much better than being back in the barracks where there was nobody I could talk to about anything of even the remotest interest to me. Of course I couldn't explain any of this to Stanley because I didn't know how, and because I was afraid he might dismiss me like some whiny kid he was tired of wasting his time on.

Later of course it became clearer to me what the real cause of my bewilderment back then had been. Stanley had stirred longings in me that I'd desperately hoped to suppress, because I regarded them as sick. He, on the other hand, seemed to take my perversity for granted, planting a kiss on my cheek as if it was the most natural thing in the world, and making jokes about my love affairs. I'd ended up close to tears because all I really wanted was for Stanley to kiss me again. Even more than that I wanted to kiss him back. That I didn't tell him at the time, that I tried to hide my feelings, is something I've regretted ever since.

5

It was not the first time that my longings, as I call them, had caused me to suffer this kind of anguish. Beginning when I was nine or ten years old I'd felt earmarked for trouble. By then I'd outgrown all of the ordinary childhood pleasures. Even now, if I try to remember a time of innocent enjoyment in the things and people around me I can't. In photographs I'm a scowling infant and child, my brow creased in a permanent furrow. Raised without brothers or sisters in a household full of secrets and silence, I'd learned very young to be secretive and silent myself. My father was a country policeman. He was also a mean drunk, a fact that made me wary of getting close to him or of relying on him for consistent support or affection. My only ally as a child had been my mother, for whom I felt a desperate affection despite my father's contention that she was a sorry excuse for a woman. It was

Doris who'd encouraged my friendship with Bill, our neighbour. She thought the sun shone out of Bill, because of his looks and his education and his beautiful voice. And it was true that, compared to my father, Bill seemed positively saintly.

So Doris was happy for me to spend most of my free time next door with him, and with his dog Molly. The two of them had first moved in with Bill's mother in 1939. I remember my first sighting of them cruising up our street in Bill's dove-grey Buick, Molly with her head stuck out of the driver's side window so that she appeared to be in control of the wheel. The next morning, as I was leaving for school, Bill had introduced himself to my mother over the top of the hedge that separated our houses and had invited her to an afternoon tea of cakes and pastries he was in the throes of baking himself.

After that I was always over there; helping him and his mother to reform their garden, assisting in the design and construction of the new kitchen Bill was building by hand—carpentry being one of his many skills. As far as I could tell he did no actual work, living off what he and his mother called their 'investments', a notion my father found deeply suspicious. Not that I cared less what my father said about my new friend. To me Bill was like a brother even though he was so much older than I was—twenty-three when I first got to know him—and I regarded him as a sun around which I could revolve forever and ever and never get burned.

I don't know exactly how or when things changed between us, but it had to do with the tennis lessons and the new camera Bill bought to take studio pictures. He was a keen photographer, as well as an athlete. I knew this from all the books he had. The whole of the downstairs, where he had his own living room, was lined with bookcases. He even had books standing on the floor in piles, most of them about photography or art or fashion, although there were novels and poetry among them too. He'd shipped them home from London, where he'd lived from the age of eighteen, studying art history and working in a few different casual jobs, the more menial the better he said.

'You'd love London,' he said. 'It's so full of life.'

His constant complaint about living back home was the deathly silence.

'Why did you leave?' I said.

'I ask myself that same question every day,' he said.

The real reason was his mother, who needed someone to keep an eye on her now that she wasn't well. His older brothers were all too busy with their own lives, according to Bill, so he'd been delegated to move back home and take on the role of nursemaid.

'I don't mind,' he said. 'I needed a rest. And anyway things in Europe were so grim.'

He taught me to take photos with an old box camera he had. And he let me develop my own prints in the dark room he'd built under the stairs, praising the results so extravagantly I blushed with pride. It was rare for anyone except Doris to tell me that I was good at anything. I took the photographs home with me and stuck them in a scrapbook in categories. There was a section for Molly and a section for trees and a section for still life. Bill had told me to see the subjects as arrangements of light and shade as well as actual objects. This became an obsession of mine for quite a long time, because it was a revelation for me to learn that our perception of even the simplest things was not fixed or straight-forward, but open to different interpretations.

I started to draw at home: cups and saucers, knives and forks, my father's shoes lined up at the laundry door waiting for me to shine them. For a teenage boy on the eve of a war I was strangely uninterested in fighter planes and battleships, all of the military machinery my school friends liked to sketch endlessly. This was probably due to a ban on such drawings from Bill, who had proclaimed himself a pacifist early on in our acquaintance, and who only got bad-tempered if I mentioned events in Europe.

'I can't bear to think about it,' he said. 'All those mad old men plotting ways to destroy another whole generation of boys.'

I made a solemn promise to him that I wouldn't join up no matter what, although secretly I'd decided on the Air Force as my preferred branch of the armed services. Mainly I suppose I was inspired by my father's scornful dismissal of fighter pilots as *degenerate dandies* compared to the common foot soldiers.

My mother saw my drawings of domestic scenes and yelped with delight. She bought me sketchbooks and pencils and encouraged me to think of a career in the arts. My father saw the drawings and said nothing. It was as if they were a foreign language he didn't understand. When I tried to explain the effects I was after he told me not to waste my breath.

A few months later I announced to my parents that I'd changed my mind about becoming a racing-car driver. I said I wanted to be a designer, although I wasn't sure yet which kind. *Maybe clothes*, I said. Bill had been teaching me to see clothes not just as clothes, but as coded messages about who you were and how you spent your time and how much money and class you had. *Never underestimate appearances*, he told me.

'Good for you,' said my mother.

'Over my dead body,' said my father.

My father didn't like Bill. He didn't like the fact that I spent so much time next door and hardly any time at home. To keep me better occupied he invented chores for me like painting the front fence and chopping logs for kindling. I was old enough, he said, to start pulling my weight around the house. When I asked for pocket money in return for my labour he slapped me hard across the side of the head.

'What was that for?' I said.

'I don't like your tone,' he said.

Another time I asked for some tennis shoes so I didn't have to play in bare feet and he told me I could forget about learning tennis because it was a game for ponces. I didn't argue back because he'd been drinking for most of the afternoon. He glared at me across the top of his whisky glass and asked me if I knew what a ponce was. I said I did.

'Tell me then,' he said. The whites of his eyes were full of tiny red veins in the shape of tree branches.

I didn't answer. I couldn't tell him that at school Brian Callaghan got the girlie boys and pulled down their pants in front of everyone to prove how small their dicks were. He'd tried to do it to me once but I'd punched him so hard in the face his nose bled. He never came near me again.

'If you have to think about it you must be lying,' said my father.

'Shirt-lifter, nancy boy, fairy,' I said. 'Same thing.'

My father licked his full, glistening lips and stared at me some more, and then he told me to get the fuck out of his sight.

My mother bought me the sandshoes with a secret stash she kept in her underwear drawer.

'Leave them at Bill's,' she told me. 'When you're not using them.'

I played tennis in secret; I took photographs in secret; I modelled for Bill's studio work without telling even Doris because Bill was worried she might get the wrong idea.

At thirteen years old I was tall for my age and starting to fill out. Bill said I looked like I might even outgrow him. On my thirteenth birthday he gave me a present of a book on anatomy for artists and he baked me an apple upside down cake. That was during the week his mother went into hospital to have surgery on her eyes, so we were alone together. After I'd eaten almost half the cake in a single sitting, he told me to stand up next to the wall where he'd kept a record of my spectacular growth over the two years I'd known him. When I was standing straight he parted my hair and made a mark on the wall with a pencil. Beside it he wrote my name and the date August 17th 1941, and then he said he wanted to show me something.

'It's a magazine about photography. I bought it in Berlin.'

'Did you ever see Hitler?' I said.

'No. But his bullyboys were everywhere. Strutting about in their tight little uniforms.'

He goose-stepped a few paces on his way to the narrow back room he called his study. I followed him and watched him fetch the magazine from the top of a tall bookcase.

'It's quite a rare item,' he said.

The magazine was in a plain brown box. There were other magazines in there too, but this was the best one, he said.

He talked about his studio, but it wasn't an actual professional studio. It was just the garage down the end of the driveway, where he kept his car. There was room for two cars there but Bill had built a partition and made a space where he could set up his lights and make scenery and props, and that's where I posed for him in various homemade costumes—sailor suits and riding kit, kilts and Roman togas. The pictures in the magazine showed men with nothing on at all, posed in front of painted mountain scenery. They were facing the front, so you could see everything. I laughed when I saw them.

'You think they're funny?' said Bill.

'Not really,' I said. 'They're very well lit.'

Bill seemed pleased with my answer.

'I was thinking of rigging up some heating in the studio,' he said. 'So we don't freeze in there.' He explained that the photographs in the magazine were for artists, so they could accurately draw the male body.

I glanced at him as he leafed through the pages. 'So you want me to pose in the nuddy next time?' I said.

'Would you mind?' he said, looking straight at me with an expression of disbelief.

'It doesn't make any difference to me,' I said, although that wasn't strictly true. In fact the idea excited me. It was where the studio photographs had been heading anyway and it didn't seem such a leap to take for me to be naked in the pictures if that was what Bill wanted. I would have done anything to please him. I tried to imitate the expressions worn by the men in the photographs, which were all a mixture of conceit and amusement. It was Bill's turn to laugh then.

'Where did you come from?' he said.

'Next door,' I said.

He put his arm around my shoulder and gave me a squeeze and I could have stayed there all day, in his firm grip, breathing in the stench of his sweat and pomade.

I once asked my mother why she hadn't married someone more like Bill, someone who was interested in the same things she was, like movies and reading, and she suddenly looked like she was about to cry. *I'm not a very good judge of men*, she said. That was true. She should never have trusted Bill for a start. I don't think she had any idea of the kind of man he was, no more than I did. She admired him, and she responded to his kindness, and I never told her anything to make her think there was a particular motive behind it, because I didn't believe there was.

Things came to a head one sunny morning in September. It was right at the end of the spring holidays, most of which I'd spent on the tennis court with Bill, trying to improve my backhand and my serve. My father must have known what I was up to but refrained from intervening because, despite his explosive temper, he was capable of restraint when it suited his purpose. After a typically silent breakfast I watched my father put on his policeman's jacket and leave for work, and then I went over to Bill's place for my lesson.

I found him in the kitchen, looking pale and shaky. My first thought was that his call-up papers had finally come, despite all his letters to the authorities regarding his pacifist convictions and his sick mother.

'What's the matter?' I said.

He told me to sit while he fetched me a cup of tea. His hand was shaking as he put the cup down in front of me.

'Two things have happened,' he said. 'The first is that Molly has gone missing.'

'Since when?' I said. 'She was here last night. I took her for her walk.'

'I know you did,' he said. He gave me a sideways look then closed his eyes.

'What's the second thing?' I said.

'Your father left a note in my letterbox,' he said.

'What does it say?'

'Terrible things,' said Bill. His eyes were open again but he wouldn't look at me. He kept staring at the surface of the kitchen table where his tea was going cold in front of him.

'Can I read it?'

'No,' he said. 'I burned it.'

He looked up as his mother came in from the front garden. With her hair uncombed and her feet bare, she looked like she'd spent the whole night outdoors.

'Anything?' he said.

She shook her head and shuffled past Bill's chair to the kitchen sink where she stood gripping the bench as if she might fall over at any minute.

Bill told me to go home but I refused. 'I'm going to look for Molly,' I said, because an idea was forming in my head about where she might be.

My father had complained to my mother before now, urging her to speak to Bill about keeping his yappy mutt chained up so she wasn't free to wander into our yard and do her business on our lawn.

'She doesn't do any harm,' my mother said.

'Well don't be surprised if I decide to drown the fucking thing the next time I catch it,' he said.

The creek was the only place he would have gone to drown a dog. I'd watched him drown kittens there once when I was smaller. He explained to me that we couldn't keep them all, only the mother and one other so she could teach it how to catch rats. All my subsequent murderous thoughts about my father had probably stemmed from the way he smiled at me that day, while he tied a piece of cord around the neck of the sack. Inside were all of the mewling kittens except the grey one. My six-year-old blood had raged and sent me flying at him, throwing punches and kicking at his shins with my little boots. After he'd hurled the sack in the creek he'd picked me up by the scruff of the neck and flung me in the water to drown along with the kittens. It was only at the last moment he'd bothered to rescue me, just before I sank. He had to carry me home across his shoulder like something he'd hunted down and shot.

After Molly's disappearance I waded along the creek bed for two hours, trying to find the sack with the small body in it, but it was no good. Whatever my father had done with her, he'd been thorough about covering his tracks. Bill found me some time later wandering like a beggar around town calling out Molly's name, asking all the shopkeepers if they'd seen her anywhere. He drove me home in the Buick, parked it in the garage and, after he'd turned off the engine, he told me that he and I couldn't be friends any more and I wasn't to come over to his house ever again.

'I'm very sorry,' he said, leaning over to kiss the top of my head.

I did as I was told. I was too scared not to, because of the way Bill had looked at me in the car, and because of what a dangerous man my father was. He came home from the station that evening and sat down at the dinner table in the usual way except that he was carrying a brown-paper parcel under one arm. After he'd settled himself in his chair he placed the parcel in front of him almost tenderly. As my mother tried to move it to make room for his dinner plate he grabbed hold of her arm and wouldn't let go.

'If you or your son ever lie to me or go behind my back again,' he said, 'I won't be answerable for the consequences. Do I make myself clear?'

He picked up the parcel and threw it at me so hard I had no time to get out of the way. It hit me in the head and split open. My tennis shoes and all the loose sand in them spilled out and fell in my food. Tied to one of the shoelaces with a little bow was five inches of Molly's tail where it had been separated from the rest of her with a knife.

When my mother went to remove my plate and pick up the shoes, my father told her to leave everything where it was. 'As for you,' he said, pointing his beefy forefinger at me, 'you will remain in your place until you've eaten every last morsel of food your mother has taken so much trouble to prepare for you.'

My mother pleaded with him. 'Don't John,' she begged. 'Let me get him a fresh serving at least.'

'If you move,' said my father. 'I'll kill you.'

It never occurred to me to tell Stanley the full facts about my friendship with Bill, not in the infirmary or later. It was a story I'd decided to take to my grave. My past was not a subject I was eager to discuss with anyone, unless it was to make it seem exceptional by embellishing the truth. When Stanley asked about my parents I told him the same lie I'd told a dozen other people, including May. I said I'd been fostered out after my mother and father had abandoned me.

'Who looked after you?' he said.

'Various people.'

'Such as?'

'A fashion designer. And after that an architect.'

We were sitting in the reading room on the last evening before he was taken back into camp. He was sorting out his few possessions, the clothes and books he'd brought with him in his pitiful suitcase. It was covered in tattered stickers and labels from all the places he'd stayed on his travels.

'Have you spent much time in Japan?' I said, trying to draw him out since I imagined I might never get another chance.

'No.'

'What about your parents?'

'What about them?' he said.

'Have they spent a lot of time in Japan?'

'I guess,' he said. 'They're Japs.'

I asked him if he'd like me to go back to my room.

'No,' he said. 'When I want you to go back to your room I'll tell you.'

And then he smiled at me and said he was sorry for being so rude, but that his family was too dull to talk about. At the same time he cupped his hand to his ear as if he was straining to catch a faint sound in the distance.

'Can you hear that wailing sound coming from Hut C12?' he said. 'That's my mother talking to my father. Droning on and on about how brainless I am.'

'I thought your father wasn't here,' I said.

'Tell that to my mother,' he said, pointing to his temple and drawing circles there to indicate that his mother was crazy. I was prepared to believe it, having seen her for myself.

While he tried on a pair of his trousers to see if they still fitted I picked up one of his circus posters. He was in the picture, aged about ten, standing at the front of a row of men in their circus outfits, the tallest of whom bore an unmistakable resemblance to Stanley.

'Is that your father?' I asked him.

'Yep,' he said, clearly unwilling to say any more.

He took off the trousers and folded them neatly while I stared at his legs. They were practically hairless and the same ivory white as the rest of him. Aware of me watching him, he struck a couple of poses as if he was a batter warming up at the plate. When he'd finished teasing me, he reached out and plucked the poster out of my hands. He stared briefly at it before rolling it up with the others and packing it in his suitcase.

I picked up one of his books from the pile on the sofa beside me and opened it in the normal way. Stanley grabbed it from me and demonstrated, as if to a child, how it opened from the back.

'It's different from English,' he said.

'I can see that,' I said, staring at a random page of densely packed symbols cascading like rain from top to bottom.

I asked him to read aloud to me.

'What for?' he said almost viciously.

'Don't bother if it's too much trouble,' I said.

He snatched the book out of my hands again and opened it somewhere in the middle, holding it at a distance from his body, as if it were a holy book. He cleared his throat and started to intone sentences in Japanese, adding occasional gestures with his free hand that were meant to signify blessings. Even though it was intended to be funny it still moved me in the way that even nonsense words can if they're said in a certain rhythm and at a certain pitch. When he was finished with one page he made a sign and turned to the next and then he sped up the process so that he was flicking through the pages at impossible speed, still reading, but so fast that the words were jumbled and mashed together. Finally, when he'd reached the last page, he sent the book sailing out of his hand, so that it landed with a thud halfway across the room.

His performance over Stanley fell backwards onto the sofa exhausted. 'Give me a fag before I die of grief,' he said, pretending to wipe the sweat from his brow.

I handed him the matchbox in which he kept his butts and

watched him light one. 'Great story,' I said.

'Glad you enjoyed it,' said Stanley. 'Akutagawa again. He's a genius of course.'

'Of course,' I said. 'I can tell.'

Stanley offered me a drag on his smoke. I took it and sucked hard. He watched the tip of it burn hot then drop a length of ash on the floor.

'Don't smoke it all,' he said.

'I can get you as many cigarettes as you want once I'm out of here,' I said.

I crawled across the floor, picked up the book and handed it back to him.

'I can't wait to read more,' I said.

Stanley smiled at me coolly and told me I could go back to my room now. He said it in such a way that I had no option but to obey.

I got up off the floor and padded back to my own bed where I lay for a long time staring at a narrow beam of light that stretched all the way from Stanley's room to my doorway. The fine dust swirled backwards and forwards through it like flurries of snow. I was worried that I might have offended Stanley without meaning to, but I had no idea how to apologise, or even if it was worthwhile to try.

This idea, that our acquaintance was over before it had really begun, made me anxious and miserable. I thought of getting up again to say goodbye to him in a formal way but I wasn't sure if he would appreciate a further interruption to his preparations. In the end I stayed where I was and drifted in and out of a shallow sleep, imagining at times that I was back in Bill's house searching high and low for him. When my parents came to get me I sat them down at the kitchen table and told them I was leaving them for good to be with Bill. *I love him*, I remember telling them in my dreams, and being surprised that neither of them was angry or shocked.

The next morning Stanley came into my room dressed and ready to leave. He had the book in his hand, the one he'd read from the previous night. Without saying a word he came to my bedside and handed it to me, then he bowed very low before turning around to leave. It was all so swift I didn't have time to say good morning or to thank him and anyway I suspected I would have choked on the words. After he was gone I opened the book and saw what Stanley had written inside the cover. *Dear Arthur, I will try to write Akutagawa in English for you if you will get me the fags you promised, your good friend Stanley Ueno.* Below that he'd written something in Japanese that naturally I couldn't read. In brackets beside it he'd written *Untranslatable.*

6

Two days later I left the infirmary myself. I wasn't completely well, but at least I was able to eat without becoming nauseous and Matron Conlon advised that if I avoided salty foods and took proper rest I should continue to improve. For the headaches she recommended Bex tablets, as many as required to dull the pain. They were harmless, she said, *like sweeties*. She also told me to drink alcohol, because it was such a tried and trusted cure for nerves.

'Not too much mind,' she said. 'But a tipple now and then never hurt a fly.'

I tried to settle back into my former life, rising before dawn, donning my ugly uniform, carrying out my duties with the minimum of fuss. I showered and ate my meals with men who treated me like the village idiot, and bunked down at night in the cold and draughty hut I shared with three other soldiers, Donohue, Bryant and McMaster, enduring their constant jibes at my youth and inexperience. It wasn't easy. The other men all had an aptitude for military life, whereas I had none. I was only in the army because of a fluke meeting on a Melbourne tram with an old school friend to whom I'd told a pack of lies about my abrupt exit from the Air Force. Out of sympathy for my troubles he'd advised me where to go if I wanted to get back into uniform, and I was grateful, because anything was preferable to being a civilian. Being a civilian meant constant harassment from strangers wanting to know why a strapping young man like myself wasn't on the front line somewhere doing his patriotic duty instead of swanning down Collins Street in a spivvy suit. It wore you down. In the end you felt like George Orwell in the elephant story, capable of any folly as long as it saved you from looking like a fool.

Coming so late to the camp, and being so young, I'd struggled to fit in at Tatura. All the other guards were in their forties. Most of them had been in the last war and had missed the army enough to volunteer a second time round as soon as the call came. They reminded me of my father, in that the 1914 war had turned them into troubled, unsympathetic loners. Life as a Tatura guard seemed to suit a certain personality type—incurious, cynical, sentimental—all traits that I recognised from growing up in my father's field of gravity.

Luckily, however, there were some exceptions. Riley, for example, turned out to be a true friend, even if at first meeting I found him difficult to like. He shared none of my views on the Japs and told me so in no uncertain terms.

'You don't want to believe everything you read in the papers son,' he said. 'The first casualty of war, as the saying goes.'

This was on my first day on duty back in April, before I'd fallen ill. Riley had been assigned to give me a tour of the camp and fill me in on its workings, but it seemed as if his main purpose was to discourage me from thinking my job would make any real contribution to the war effort.

'We're running an asylum,' he told me. 'The patients are all perfectly sane people and our job is to drive them crazy.'

'How do we do that?' I said, uncertain how seriously I was meant to take him, given that his manner was so unmilitary. He talked to me like we were taking a stroll through a holiday resort. I didn't know whether to be disappointed or relieved, such was my confusion back then. I was still in a state of shock at the sheer size of the camp and at the numbers of Japs it housed. I estimated there were about eight hundred of them, which seemed to me like a dangerously large number to be concentrated in one place.

'Countless ingenious schemes,' he said. 'We encourage them to do useful work. We even pay them for their labours. Then we take the money back when they want cigarettes or postage stamps.'

To illustrate the point he took me through the clothing factory, a long low corrugated-iron hut running parallel to the mess hall, where about fifty women sat making new clothes out of old ones. Most of them were sewing by hand, but some were sitting at antiquated machines. They all paused to watch us pass by. Some of them even smiled and called out to Riley to give them free fags in exchange for a kiss. *You so handsome* they cried. Riley might have been handsome once but his stocky body was running to fat and his skin was leathery from too much sun. He laughed at the women and told them he'd have to decline the offer. If he kissed one of them, he said, the others would all want a kiss too, and then he'd spend his whole day kissing girls, which would more than likely kill him. He seemed to know them all by name, and the names of their children, some of whom had decided to follow us around in a little pack.

'A new guard's a novelty to them,' he said. 'Especially one who hasn't started shaving.'

It unnerved me the way I was shadowed. One or two of the smaller children even wanted to hold my hand briefly before running back to the pack. It all seemed over-friendly to me. I flinched whenever one of them came near me and was careful to keep my hands in my pockets.

After the factory visit Riley walked me along the high perimeter fences that formed the boundary of the camp. I remember him pointing to an invisible line in the dust just inside the inner fence and explaining the three-yard rule to me.

'We promise not to shoot them if they stay this side of that line,' he said.

I tried to make out a mark in the dirt. 'I don't see it,' I said.

'It must be there,' he said, 'because there hasn't been a shot fired in the three years I've been in the camp.'

He pointed to the watchtower up ahead, where two half-mile lengths of the outer fence joined up and where a manned machine-gun was installed for everyone to see. He waved to the gunner, who waved back.

'It's doubtful if the guns up there even work,' he said.

I'd counted five watchtowers in all, one at each corner of the perimeter and one at the main gate. I wondered if he meant none of the guns worked or only the one nearest to where we were standing.

'No need to look so worried,' he said, slapping me hard on the shoulder. 'Just so you know you're not in any danger from friendly fire.'

He told me the only thing I would have to really watch out for were the nippers. He said this in a loud voice for the amusement of the half-dozen or so children who were still following behind us as we walked along. I'd glanced back a couple of times and caught one of them mimicking my gait. If you were watching very carefully you could tell that I continued to favour my busted ankle, even though it had completely healed.

'Especially that little blackfella Thompson,' said Riley, still talking loudly.

I glanced around again and saw he meant the mimic, a skinny kid of about eight, who had dissolved into a fit of giggles as soon as his name was mentioned. I glared at him to make him stop what he was doing but he took no notice of me. As soon as my back was turned he continued to trail along behind me with his right foot hitching up in an exaggerated limp.

'Why are there blackfellas here?' I said.

'There's some of them married to Japs,' said Riley. 'So it's guilt by association. Their dads were generally pearlers up north, or canecutters. Thompson's real name is Tomioka.'

At lunchtime, in the mess hall, he pointed out how the different groupings tended to stick together. 'The Darwin mob are very tight,' he said. 'A lot of them are related one way or another. Same with the New Caledonians and the Formosans.'

'Where are all the men?' I said. Apart from teenage boys and old men, the hall seemed to be filled with women and children.

'We used to have a lot more men here,' said Riley, 'but then they reclassified all the seamen as a security risk and sent them to Hay. So what you see here is the lonely wives' club.'

While he was talking he walked me around from table to table and introduced me, just as if I was the new boy at school.

'Be nice to him,' he told everyone. 'He's just a kiddie.'

This made my face redden and I started to sweat inside my uniform even though it was as cold in the hall as it was outside on the parade ground. I had reason to be nervous because I'd never seen so many foreign faces in one place before and it was frightening to be so plainly outnumbered. Everyone was polite enough but I sensed that I was an object of amusement, rather than of any real respect, and I resented this deeply because it somehow confirmed my feeling of general ineptitude.

'Very pretty boy,' said one of the women, who was helping to clear away the dirty dishes and wipe the tables.

'You keep your hands off him,' said Riley, smiling; then he spoke to her in French and she screamed with laughter.

'You very naughty,' she told Riley.

'Not me luv,' said Riley. 'I'm one of the good ones.'

Before we left the mess, Riley took me across and introduced me to a group of about a dozen young boys who were sitting at one of the tables furthest away from the doors. They were all dressed in black and I wondered if this was some kind of rule. As well as that, they all had closely shaved hair, which made them look like boy monks; the oldest amongst them was probably no more than thirteen. Riley knew each of their names and called on them one by one to say hello to me. Without looking up from their plates they took it in turns to mutter, 'Hello Private Wheeler.'

'Keeping your noses clean?' said Riley, when they'd all done as he'd asked.

There was no answer.

'You better be,' said Riley. 'Because you're being watched.'

A couple of the boys glanced up at him. The others stared sullenly at their food as if it had suddenly lost its flavour. The oldest-looking boy spoke just as we were leaving.

'You're wasting your time,' he said.

'I sincerely hope so, son,' said Riley, giving the boy a cheery wave meant to make him laugh. Except that it had the opposite effect. The boy scowled at us and said something in Japanese under his breath.

Riley ignored him and led me away.

'What did he just say?' I said.

'*Baka*,' said Riley.

'What does it mean?'

'It's the worst swear word in the Japanese language,' he said. 'It means idiot, or fool.'

'And that's as bad as it gets?' I said.

'Very easy to insult a Jap,' said Riley. 'You don't need a big vocabulary.'

Over lunch in the guards' mess he told me the boys in black had been mixed up in a knife fight a few weeks before my arrival.

'Nothing serious,' he said, 'a few cuts and abrasions. The insti-gator was a kid named Sawada, who in my opinion doesn't belong here. He needs packing off to the single-men's camp without delay.'

'Is he the one who swore at you?' I said.

'No,' said Riley. 'The boy I'm talking about is in the lock-up, where he spends half his life. If it wasn't for the fact that he's still a minor he'd be gone from here.'

'What's he in the lock-up for?'

Riley told me that Sawada had built a radio and kept it hidden in his hut for months until his mother found it and turned him in. 'So he beat her over the head with a chair leg. And not for the first time.'

I watched Riley eat his food. I'd left mine untouched on my plate because I'd lost my appetite.

'My theory is that they learn radio engineering in school,' said Riley. 'Did you notice the old man sitting by himself at the table near the entrance to the mess hall?'

'I wasn't paying attention.'

'Well you should,' said Riley. 'His name's Baba-san. He runs a school for the Japs to send their kids to if they want them to learn to read and write Japanese.'

'Is that allowed?' I said.

'The theory is that it keeps them occupied,' said Riley. 'But I'll wager there's a fair amount of brainwashing goes on as well.'

'If that's true then how does he get away with it? I mean shouldn't we be trying to stop that sort of thing?'

Riley smiled at me. 'There are a lot of things we should try to put a stop to,' he said. 'If it would make a difference.'

When I asked him for a list he laughed.

'What's so funny?' I said.

'Make a flaming list yourself,' he said. 'Give us a gander when you've finished. It might make for entertaining reading.'

Looking back, I realise that Riley was warning me again not to make the mistake of taking our work at Tatura too seriously, because in essence we were guarding people who had nowhere else to go anyway and no wish to leave. As a consequence we were not really required to do very much except to act like senior prefects occasionally when someone stepped out of line. It was years before it dawned on me that the real tragedy of Tatura had been nothing to do with us anyway. It had stemmed from the clumsy and panicky way that the Japs had been lumped together and branded as traitors.

The camp commandant, a colonel by the name of Hollows, had already reached a similar conclusion by the time I met him. He ordered me to report to him at the end of my first week of duty, a prospect that terrified me, given his reputation. Riley had described him as unpredictable, sometimes kindly and at other times a martinet, so I was relieved when he welcomed me into his office in a friendly, almost familiar way, as if he already had plans for me. He told me to stand at ease then said he wanted to hear my impressions of the camp so far. I didn't answer straightaway, mainly because I'd never expected to be asked for my opinion. It was rare for a low-ranking soldier like me to be consulted on any topic whatsoever, let alone on the subject of his own observations.

I concluded that Colonel Hollows must be trying to test me in some way, that he was probing my suitability for some special task.

Eventually I came up with something I thought would please him. 'I think the camp is an excellent example of what the army does best,' I said, in my most ingratiating voice, 'which is to organise and discipline a large number of people over a long period of time for a common purpose.'

Impatience flashed across the colonel's round, moustachioed features.

'I think that's missing the point soldier,' he said.

I waited for him to continue but he went very quiet. He sat contemplating his pudgy hands for some time, then stood up from his desk and crossed to the window of his office where he stood gazing out across the parade ground to the mess hall on the other side.

And then he spoke, a little theatrically I thought, about historians of the future, and how he hoped they would recognise how vital it was to take these people in and keep them safe at a time when they were in peril from the worst elements of our society.

'Does that make sense, Wheeler?' he said, turning around to look at me. With his wide-awake eyes and whiskers he reminded me of a beaver.

'Yes sir,' I said.

To be honest it made no sense at all to me. All week I'd been wrestling with incomprehension about my duties as an enlisted man a thousand miles from danger, and now my problem had been made worse. The only thing I knew for certain was that my chances of redemption by acts of wartime valour had been finally and forever reduced to zero. It wasn't just a case of my having arrived at exactly the wrong place at exactly the wrong time; it was a case of my having blown all my chances up to this point in spectacular fashion. Before I left the colonel's office he told me that from now on I would be assisting with the children in the English-language school run by McMaster, unless I had any objections. I told him I had none, and then, as I saluted and turned to leave, I felt a stabbing pain in my stomach and knew that this was what it felt like to lose heart altogether.

That night I wrote a letter to May to tell her how lonely I was and how much I looked forward to seeing her again.

I feel like I'm going mad. I haven't had a minute to myself since I got here and there's nobody to talk to about anything except the rotten war news, which I don't enjoy hearing because it only makes me feel sorry for myself. You asked me on my last visit whether I was afraid of fighting. Actually I think I'm more afraid of not fighting. What am I going to tell my children when they ask me what I did in the war? How am I going to explain to them that I looked after a bunch of Japs and made sure they were kept happy and contented while real soldiers were out fighting and dying on the battlefield? It's sickening to think about. I've never felt so useless in my entire life. I'd rather do what you do than spend another day in this shithole (pardon the French). At least you can see a result, whereas what I do produces nothing but despair all round.

She wrote back to me and said that the censors had blacked out most of my letter except for the bit about my children. She asked me how many I wanted and what their names might be, and then suggested an ideal number would be four, two girls for her and two boys for me. Like all her other letters I kept this one under my pillow and took it out at night to re-read it when I couldn't sleep. I think it helped me to remember that there was another world outside Tatura, and also that someone out there—it didn't much matter who—was thinking of me not as a boy soldier but as a man.

7

Although I'd caught the occasional glimpse of Stanley out on parade, I hadn't been close enough to speak to him. We didn't meet face to face again until he came looking for me one day after morning roll call. This was at the end of May about ten days after we'd both left the infirmary. I'd been given leave to go into Tatura township to pick up some school supplies. I also had plans to meet May, who'd found work on a farm about a forty-minute bus ride from Shepparton. In a letter she wrote me around that time she'd described her determination to keep close by me as worthy of a medal for *dogged devotion*.

As I was leaving my hut Stanley appeared around the corner as if he'd been waiting for me. He was looking well fed and pleased with himself, and I remember he was wearing a very serviceable funeral suit with a shirt and tie. The Red Cross sent charity bins to the camp on a regular basis so Stanley had obviously helped himself. His shoes were black patent leather with some kind of animal-skin trim, and already covered in a layer of fine dust because nothing in the camp stayed dust-free for long no matter how diligent you were. The wind was to blame. It was rare to have a day when it wasn't swirling around the huts in a state of perpetual agitation.

'What are you doing here?' I said. I was hoping he couldn't see me blushing. I fiddled with the doorhandle, pretending it was stiff.

'It's a free country,' he said.

'Not for you it isn't,' I said.

He smiled but I could tell that he didn't think the joke was very funny. Then he asked me about my health and I told him I was feeling much better.

'Nice shoes,' I said.

He looked down at his new shoes then rubbed them on the back of his pant legs.

'Good for dancing,' he said and did a little soft-shoe shuffle towards me.

When he was closer he stopped dancing and put his hand inside his jacket pocket. I half-expected him to produce a knife, as proof that he was ready to take me on again if I wanted to fight him, but instead he pulled out a piece of folded paper and offered it to me with a quick bow. I took it from him and opened it out. Three sheets of paper were stuck together end to end like a scroll, then creased into a concertina. At the top he'd written *The Spider Thread, by Ryunosuke Akutagawa,* and underneath he'd written out the whole story in English. In the margins he'd drawn illustrations in pen and ink.

'That's a lot of work,' I said.

He didn't respond. He still hadn't really looked at me. He kept glancing around to make sure nobody had spotted him standing there. In his black suit and matching tie he looked like a mobster, an effect he'd no doubt intended.

'Can you get me some smokes?' he said. He reached into his pants pocket and pulled out a few coins, which he proceeded to count.

'I don't need payment,' I said. I took out the packet of smokes I had on me and handed it to him.

'Thanks for the story,' I said. 'I'm sure it's a masterpiece.' I shoved the pages into my coat pocket.

'I wrote it from memory,' he said. 'I've read it a hundred times.'

And then we just stood there not knowing what else to say. It wasn't the way it had been in the infirmary. Now we were back in the camp I was far more afraid than I had been before, and so was Stanley. I could tell by the way his hands trembled as he took out a fag and attempted to light it. Eventually I had to help him to hold the flame steady and shelter it from the wind. I cupped my hands around his for the few seconds it took for the cigarette to catch then slipped them back in my pockets feigning nonchalance.

'All dressed up and nowhere to go,' I said, glancing at his handsome suit.

He raised himself up on his toes and danced another couple of steps.

'They didn't send you back to Ballarat then?'

'I refused to go,' he said, finally turning to look me in the face, his smile broadening into a grin.

'What do you do all day?' I said.

'Plan my next escape,' he said, pushing the hair back off his forehead in a gesture that made my heart alter its rhythm.

'I thought you decided there wasn't any point,' I said.

'Doesn't mean I can't dream,' he said.

He asked me if I was still teaching at the school and I said I was.

'How's that going?' he said.

'Passes the time,' I said. 'You should come round one day.'

'What for?'

'Help me sharpen pencils.'

He took a long drag on his cigarette and glanced around again to check that we weren't being watched.

'When?' he said.

'Whenever you like.'

'I might drop in. If I'm not too busy.'

Then he turned and walked away the same way he'd come, swinging an imaginary cane and strutting like Chaplin's little tramp for my amusement. Just before he disappeared around the corner of the hut he paused and gave me a wave with his fingers. The last I saw of him was the trail of smoke he left in his wake. As soon as the scent of it reached where I was standing I felt a feverish excitement. I hadn't really expected to run into Stanley again. I'd expected him to disappear back into his own life, and me to disappear back into mine. At the same time the two or three glimpses I'd caught of him over the past few days had left me sick with longing. I took the folded paper out of my pocket and devoured Stanley's schoolboy scrawl, expecting, I suppose, something revelatory and personal, instead of this obscure fable about a robber who is rescued from hell by the Buddha. A love letter it was not. Still I had the urge to raise the paper to my face and breathe in whatever trace remained of Stanley's odour.

I'd only just put the pages away again when Bryant, my chief tormentor, came looking for me to see if I couldn't pick up some of his contraband while I was in town.

'What's in it for me?' I said, relieved he hadn't caught me with my nose buried in Stanley's literary offering.

'A packet of fags,' he said.

'A carton,' I said. It was risky bringing stuff into the camp for Bryant. I knew that because Riley had told me.

'Christ,' said Bryant. 'You must think I'm Father fucking Christmas.'

He towered over me, his big meaty body blocking my escape route.

'Country Life,' he said.

'Camels,' I said, insisting on American smokes because I knew that would impress Stanley.

'Five packs,' he said.

'Ten,' I said, offering my hand so we could shake on the deal.

To my surprise he took it and gripped it firmly, leering at me like I'd somehow gone up in his estimation.

'Nice doing business with you,' he said.

'Likewise,' I said, trying to pull my hand free, and finally succeeding.

'Not a word to anyone,' said Bryant.

'My lips are sealed,' I said.

May read the story when I showed it to her and laughed at the mistakes in spelling and grammar. Even so I could tell she was impressed.

'Who is he?' she said. 'Where did he learn to write?'

I told her what Matron Conlon had told me, that Stanley had grown up in America while his family was touring. 'He speaks just like a Yank,' I said.

'I saw them perform just before the war broke out,' said May, folding the paper up again. 'They came to Melbourne with Wirth's Circus.'

Then she told me how her missing brother Owen had been so obsessed with the Jap tightrope walker that he'd spent days in the yard trying to learn how to keep his balance.

'He started out on a long plank of wood set up between two chairs, then he decided to string a rope between two trees and walk along it with two sticks like ski poles to stop himself from falling. In the end he managed to throw the sticks away. He was like that. He could do anything he set his mind to.'

She cried every time she talked about Owen. I was used to it. Tears would start to roll down her cheeks and she would wipe them away, at the same time her whole face would turn a blotchy red. I could never just sit there and do nothing. I always tried to comfort her, and this was how we started kissing that day, in the sitting room of the house where she was staying. It belonged to a farmer's wife who was struggling to keep the farm going while her husband was away at the war. The farmer's wife was out for the day, visiting a neighbour, so we had the place to ourselves. May had made me some scones and there was fresh cream from the cows. When we'd eaten she opened up the grog cabinet and poured us both a brandy.

'Do you want to see my room?' she said, after the brandy had done its work.

I followed her down the hallway to the back of the house and into her bedroom. She shut the door behind me. There was nothing in the room except a narrow bed and a wardrobe, but it was cheery enough and the sun was pouring in, making it warmer than the rest of the house. I remember the cat had followed us in and positioned itself on the windowsill where it sat up and watched us fumble with each other's clothing. After that there wasn't much to see. It was all over very fast. We didn't even lie down on the bed. One minute we were kissing. The next I was kneading May's big freckled breasts while she unbuttoned my pants and directed me where to put my prick. It wasn't as if I already knew, because I didn't. May and I had done a lot of feeling up and fondling, but I'd never seen a girl down there so I needed help.

'It's all right,' she kept saying. 'Do it. It's all right.'

So I did it, up against the back of the door, and was immediately sorry, not because it felt bad, but because it felt dirty. I turned away and pulled up my pants and all the time the cat stared at me out of its sly green eyes, blinking occasionally in an uneven way as if its internal mechanism was winding down.

'I'm sorry,' I said. 'That was terrible.'

May took my hand and pulled me over to the bed where she made me lie down next to her.

'It was fine,' she said.

She propped herself up on one elbow and gazed at me.

'What?' I said.

'I was just trying to imagine what you look like with all your clothes off.'

She reached across and started to unbutton my shirt, but I stopped her.

'Another time,' I said. 'I have to get my bus.'

'It's nothing to be ashamed of,' she said. 'We're all born naked.'

'Not me,' I said. 'I had my pants on.'

May gave me a little slap on the cheek.

'Liar,' she said.

'I think I need another brandy,' I said.

May got up off the bed and opened the door. In her bare feet she walked me back down the hallway to the kitchen where she'd wrapped some scones for me to take back to camp. The bottle of brandy was where she'd left it beside our teacups. She poured us each a measure, adding a generous dollop of cream and we sat at the kitchen table and spooned up our drinks like children who'd exhausted their limited supply of conversation topics. After what had happened I found I couldn't look at anything but the floor, so eventually May came around to sit next to me and took my face in both hands.

'You look like somebody died,' she said.

I stared at the scones and couldn't think of what to say. I should have told her the whole story about Stanley, about how I'd climbed into his bed in the infirmary and how he'd kissed me on the cheek. I should have said that I found it impossible to get his kiss out of my mind, and that even as I was fucking her against the back of her bedroom door I was thinking of him, remembering his smell and the shape of his earlobe. But instead I put my arms around her and gave her a hug and breathed the scent of her cheap perfume and talcum powder. I had never minded it before because of the memories of my mother, but now it gave me a panicky feeling in my stomach as if I was about to be shot.

'When are you coming again?' she said, after I'd opened the back door. I was halfway out onto the porch.

'I'll write to you,' I said. 'Let you know.'

'I'm making a new dress,' she said. 'I can show it to you the next time.'

'Send me a picture,' I said.

She came out onto the back steps and waved me goodbye. As I walked down the road back towards the highway I could feel her still watching me. When I came to the cattle grid, about a hundred yards from the house, I broke into a run and sprinted all the way to the bus stop. It wasn't until I sat down to wait for the bus that I realised I'd left the scones behind, but by then it was too late to go back and get them.

On the bus back to town, I was filled with an uneasy sense of having crossed a line. Of course a part of me was pleased, because now I was officially a man. With May's blessing I'd done the thing that needed to be done to demonstrate my virility. On the other hand, another part of me was unhappy at how I'd deceived May so easily, faked something I didn't feel. It was to be the start of years of deception, first with her and after that with other women. May would tell me, many years later, that she'd always known I was not the man I seemed to be, but that she'd loved me regardless.

'You were like a rabbit in the headlights,' she said. 'I found it irresistible.'

'Poor May,' I said.

'Your loss,' she said.

At the time that struck me as the wisest thing I'd ever heard her say.

'I'll put that on your tombstone,' I said.

'Not if you die first.'

I said I was already dead, just refusing to lie down. It was an old joke, and not especially funny. I'd been saying the same thing for years, in an attempt, I suppose, to ward off the common complaint that I was cold-hearted and remote.

May had the good grace to laugh at it every time.

8

McMaster's school was seeing a period of growth in the winter of 1945. He'd started out two years beforehand with about ten children and now there were three times that number, all crammed into a single airless room originally designed as a storeroom. A former country schoolteacher, McMaster had applied himself tirelessly to the task of building up the school from nothing. He'd written the textbooks, he'd designed the curriculum, he'd begged and borrowed equipment from wherever he could find it. He'd recently expanded the vegetable garden to twice its former size and introduced formal lessons in horticulture. But he didn't think that was the reason for the swelling numbers of students. He put the change down to the fact that the war had turned so decisively against the Japs, and that the Americans seemed willing to stop at nothing in order to win it.

'The Japs are starting to see the writing on the wall,' McMaster told me. 'And it isn't good news.'

Now that I knew him better, I could tell that his teasing back in our hut was not meant to be cruel, that to him I was just a kid not much older than his pupils.

'They're starting to think it might be wise to switch sides,' he said.

We were setting the classroom to rights at the end of a morning's teaching. McMaster liked to keep things clean and tidy. *I run a tight ship* he used to tell me at least once a day. Sometimes he'd ruffle my hair as he said it, even though I'd asked him not to.

'What's going to happen to the internees once the war's over?' I asked.

'It's anyone's guess,' said McMaster.

'Is it true they might all be shot?'

'Who told you that?'

'I've heard rumours,' I said. 'Davies seems to think some kind of revenge is on the cards.'

Davies was a guard I played chess with sometimes. He was of the firm opinion that the Japs, without exception, deserved everything they had coming to them.

'It's very unlikely,' said McMaster. 'They'll ship them all back to Japan before they waste good ammunition on them. Let them starve to death back in their own country.'

I was upset at the idea. Now that I'd met Stanley I'd been forced to reconsider my views on many things.

'Do you think any of them will be allowed to stay?' I said.

'It's possible,' he said. 'We can only hope that compassion wins out over expediency.'

McMaster was like Riley. He had no hard feelings against the Japs at Tatura. He counted some of them as friends. The rest he felt sorry for because he didn't see why they were being punished for a crime they had never committed. He liked to lecture me about the legalities of the case while we marked arithmetic tests, or typed up handouts for English homework.

'Not one shred of evidence was ever found,' he said, 'to link any of these people with any act of sabotage or any breach of national security. The crime was ours alone. Worse still it was committed in the name of liberty and justice.'

'So you're saying we should have waited until all of them had been tried in a court before we locked them up?'

'I'm saying we should never have arrested them in the first place,' said McMaster.

'Even the ones who think the Emperor is a god?'

'Since when is magical thinking a crime? A lot of people I know believe in the virgin birth. My mother's one of them. Maybe she should be arrested?'

'That's religion,' I said. 'Your mother didn't start a war in the name of the Virgin Mary.'

'Something she regrets to this day,' he said.

When he found out I played tennis McMaster asked me to run lessons after school since there was a court and some basic equipment but not many of the kids knew how to play. My tennis club proved so popular that within a fortnight of its launch I had the whole school population, plus stragglers, showing up every day. It was too many to handle on my own so I had a couple of the older kids ask around for someone in the camp who might volunteer to help me.

'Preferably someone who's played before,' I said. 'Otherwise it's the blind leading the blind.'

Soon after that Stanley showed up in his whites, with a few extra acolytes, and three tennis racquets he'd acquired from some mysterious source.

McMaster took one look at him and laughed.

'Christ,' he said. 'It's not Wimbledon.'

Stanley smiled vainly.

'I play better when I'm properly dressed,' he said. 'It gives me a mental advantage.' Then he made a show of touching his toes and stretching his neck muscles, which I gathered was for my benefit because he kept glancing at me and pouting in a ridiculous way.

McMaster already knew Stanley. He had a certain notoriety in the camp because of his famous family. Not that they were universally popular, but in the intricate tribal world of Tatura Stanley's clan—three uncles, two aunts, his mother and a cousin—seemed to have achieved respect in some quarters, and Stanley must have used this to foster his own reputation.

After he'd finished his stretches, he challenged me to an exhibition match. 'Show them how it's done,' he said, smirking.

'I thought you didn't like tennis,' I said.

'I lied,' said Stanley. 'Let's play a set after the kids' lessons? A set every afternoon until the end of the week. Best of five sets wins.'

Of course I agreed, because it gave us a reason to meet. Stanley, on the other hand seemed more concerned to prove to everyone, me especially, that he was a decent player.

McMaster was the umpire for our matches and, in the absence of a fence around the court, the kids were kept busy retrieving the balls. I was surprised to find that some of them at least were on my side. Perhaps they felt sorry for me, since it was pretty clear from the outset that Stanley was determined to beat me. He'd deceived me about his tennis game, a discovery that undermined my confidence right from the start. As the week went by my loyal supporters despaired.

'You need to get more first serves in,' said one of the boys, a clingy kid called Morisaki—Mo for short.

'I know,' I said. I was sitting next to him at one of the desks, trying to show him all the steps in a long division sum that was giving him trouble. He was small for his age and wore trademark glasses held on with elastic. But he was bright and I was beginning to enjoy teaching him and the others like him, the ones who wanted so desperately to learn that they would arrive at the schoolroom door an hour early every morning with questions about their homework.

'And you need to run faster,' he said.

'Did I ask for your help?' I said, sounding angrier than I'd intended. Mo hunched over his work and refused to say another word.

Nevertheless, I remembered his advice, and on the Friday I managed to break Stanley's serve twice and take the set. Not that it made any difference to the final result. Stanley had already won the first four matches with depressing ease. We shook hands over the net as usual and Stanley slapped me hard on the back.

'I let you have that last one,' he said. 'I could tell you were a bit out of form.' He spoke loud enough for everyone to hear.

Within seconds, Mo was by my side patting my arm because he couldn't reach my shoulder and telling me how well I'd played.

'He beat you fair and square,' he told Stanley.

Stanley laughed at him and tried to muss his hair but Mo ducked out of the way, offended.

'Somebody loves you,' said Stanley, grinning at me.

I wanted so badly to kiss him at that moment that I had to look away.

All week I'd been tormented in this fashion. The tennis had become secondary to my obsessive fantasising about what I would do to Stanley the next time we were alone together. The reason I watched the clock all day in a state of nervous anticipation was because I knew Stanley would make his appearance at three o'clock sharp, and that if I was lucky I could watch him through the window of the classroom while the kids packed up their exercise books and streamed out the door. Before the kids' tennis lessons started he liked to position a couple of boys up one end of the court and practise serving to them. This gave me five minutes to admire the fluid way he moved, the easy way he sent the ball up above his head then came over it with deadly force. It was a thrilling thing to watch. It put me in mind of Bill and I couldn't help feeling an absurd longing to somehow introduce Stanley to my old friend, offer him up as a true talent, in contrast to my occasional flashes of brilliance. It also made me wonder if

Bill had been merely flattering me all along, in order to enslave me. I remembered the pleasure it had given me as a boy, to be watched so closely and praised so fulsomely, and I understood finally that it had not been strictly for my tennis.

Even while I played against Stanley I was distracted by the sight of him: he had the habit of pushing his hair back off his forehead, and of wiping his palms one by one on his shirt. His gestures often caused me to lose sight of the ball when it came at me and I ended up wrong-footed. Of course Mo was right, I did need to run faster, but that was missing the point of the whole exercise, which was to gaze at Stanley, to drink in the look of him as if it was a drug. Whenever we changed ends I made sure to brush past Stanley's arm in what seemed a casual way, only to break out into a feverish sweat every time, as if I'd stepped too close to the edge of a drop.

I was almost glad when Stanley failed to come back the following week, because that meant I could have a respite from the agonising ritual of waiting for him. But I soon found that his absence was a worse torment than his presence. The children missed him too, and complained that the tennis lessons were overcrowded and chaotic without him there to help maintain order.

'Then ask him to come back,' I said. 'Tell him I want a re-match.'

They did as they were told and reported back that Stanley didn't want to talk to them.

'Why not?' I said.

'He's too busy.'

Whatever he was busy with it seemed to have brought about one of Stanley's changes of mood. Later I realised that nobody in the camp was immune from these shifts in the emotional temperature, not even the children. Their attitude could alter from one day to the next, depending on what they'd heard discussed the previous evening in the mess hall, or after lights out in the huts. The battle of Okinawa had been raging since April. Now it was June. News of the unprecedented brutality of the fighting had got through to everyone in some form or another, mostly as rumour and hearsay. It was like an undertow to everything that happened on the surface of their lives, moving silently but with irresistible force, dragging everybody along with it.

The next time I saw Stanley he was a changed man. He called by the schoolroom during morning lessons, coming in by the side door and pausing to listen to McMaster's class. I was at the back of the classroom stapling pages to make some lesson books for the younger kids. As soon as I caught sight of him I sensed the difference. There was a sullenness that hadn't been there before. He came over to where I was sitting and stood next to me in a sulk, his gaze fixed on a point somewhere on the wall about a foot away from my left ear. He had his funeral suit on again, and he'd found a hat to match it, a newish Homburg that he kept touching and tugging at to make sure the brim remained at the proper angle. His dancing shoes were muddy.

He asked me what I was doing and I showed him. Out the front of the class McMaster was in the middle of a talk about the history of the Royal Navy and how it had always been the real power behind the English throne.

'I won't be coming to play tennis again,' Stanley announced to no one in particular. 'It's a waste of time.'

McMaster stopped in mid-sentence and scowled at him.

In order to rescue the situation I took Stanley by the arm and led him out the door so we could talk in private, and so I could look at him properly.

'Why say that in front of everyone?' I said.

'Say what?' said Stanley. He was seething with unfocused rage. I could tell by the way he snatched the Camels I handed to him.

'That it's a waste of time,' I said. 'It's better than nothing.'

'No it's not,' said Stanley. 'It's worse.'

He took a cigarette out of the new pack and lit it without offering me one.

'Why did you tell me you hated tennis?' I said. 'You're a natural.'

He stared at the burning tip of his fag and scowled as if the sight of it was somehow enraging.

'You don't know the first thing about me,' he said.

I couldn't tell if he meant this to be a simple statement of fact or a provocation.

'I'm sorry,' I said. 'My mistake.'

He leaned his head right back and exhaled a cloud of smoke upwards into the air where it was immediately sucked away.

'What's the point in teaching them all that?' he said.

'All what?' I said.

'All that stuff about England.'

'It's history.'

'It's rubbish. History is what's happening out there.' He gestured to the empty paddocks on the other side of the fence. 'Don't you worry that the whole thing'll be over before you've had a chance to actually *do* anything?'

'All the time,' I said, gazing at him. I wanted to reach out and touch him, but then I remembered the time I'd tried to comfort him back at the infirmary and he'd fobbed me off so forcefully.

He didn't say anything for a moment, just kicked the dust with his patent leather shoes and blew puffs of smoke out the side of his mouth. When he did speak I could hardly hear what he was saying.

'I'm planning something,' he said. 'But I can't tell you what it is.'

'Loose lips sink ships,' I said, trying to provoke a smile, or some sign that the old Stanley was still there underneath this new mask.

'We can't meet again,' he said, still whispering. 'Not until this is all over and we can have a proper conversation.'

'I don't know what you mean,' I said, lowering my voice too. I was worried now that he was up to something unlawful, something that would get him into real trouble. 'What's a proper conversation?'

He stared at me then with that scornful expression he had.

'If you don't know that you're an idiot,' he said.

'Thanks,' I said sourly.

And then he walked off abruptly without saying goodbye and I was left standing there in the cold wondering what I'd done to make him loathe me so much. If it hadn't start to rain again at that moment I think I might have stayed out there for the rest of the morning, puzzling over Stanley's change of heart. He seemed to have turned overnight from a kind of frivolous dilettante into a hard case. I came inside to get out of the wet and found the mood of the room had darkened in my absence, and that one of the older children was crying.

'I'm sorry,' I said, looking at McMaster to come to my aid, although I could tell that he was just as puzzled as I was. 'We'll just have to find someone else who can help out with the tennis.'

McMaster looked across to the girl who was crying.

'What's the matter?' he asked her.

'I don't know,' she said, in a voice that was surprisingly composed. 'I'm just sad all the time for no reason.'

The other kids stared at her without speaking.

McMaster surveyed their solemn faces. 'Is there anybody else who feels the same way?' he said.

Nobody said a word. The children sat motionless at their benches, now gazing at the blackboard as if the answer to his question might suddenly appear up there like a coded message hidden in his loopy handwriting. McMaster liked to start each day by writing some pithy quotation up on the board for the children to copy into their books and think about for homework. That day he'd chosen a quote from his favourite writer, H. G. Wells. It read *History is more and more a race between education and catastrophe*. The children scrutinised the words now with a look of uniform bafflement.

9

Stanley had meant what he said. I didn't see him again because he vanished, not literally, but in the sense that the person I'd known disappeared and was replaced with someone I barely recognised. I saw this new person on the parade ground ten days or so after Stanley had formally quit the tennis club. He was standing with the little gang of Baba-san's boys while they waited for the head count to finish. The July day was freezing but Stanley and his new friends all stood stiffly to attention in their thin black shirts. They were coatless and hatless, their bare heads pale and smooth as a row of melons. Stanley was the tallest of them. I was shocked to see that he'd shaved off his hair and adopted the gang's ragtag uniform. He'd reformed the way he stood and the way he moved, in order to make himself more soldierly. When parade was dismissed, he took up the rear behind a boy who was barely half his size, copying the smaller boy's strut. My first reaction was to laugh but when the little troop came closer I stopped and tried to look soldierly myself. I'd known boys like this at school, wild-eyed and bent on trouble. I knew it was a mistake to provoke them. When Stanley passed by I stared at him, hoping to shame him, I suppose, but he ignored me so completely it was as if I wasn't there.

Stanley had nothing in common with those boys as far as I could tell. They were all what McMaster called Jap-Japs, meaning they'd been educated in Japan before the war and had imbibed a lot of that country's colourful mythology. According to McMaster, Baba-san's role as the Jap-Japs' schoolmaster and their spiritual leader was to keep their patriotic thoughts pure, unsullied by foreign influences, unmoved by all the lies and blasphemy that foreigners liked to spread about the ultimate outcome of the war. Baba-san reportedly encouraged the boys to think of themselves as future warriors, willing to go down in flames for their Emperor. McMaster's theory about Stanley's defection was that it should have been no surprise to anyone because a boy of Stanley's disposition finally had nowhere else to go. He said as much one night back in barracks when we were discussing his character.

'What do you mean?' I said. 'What kind of disposition does he have?'

McMaster had been observing Stanley for longer than I had. He was bound to know more than I did about the evolution of Stanley's personality.

'It didn't surprise me that the boarding school experiment failed,' he said. 'It was a foregone conclusion. He's never fitted in here, so why would it be any different anywhere else?'

We were playing poker after lights out with Donohue and Bryant.

'Mainly because he's a pansy,' muttered Donohue, who was on a winning streak and kept on smiling to himself.

McMaster looked at me over the top of his cards. 'I suspect he's like you in that regard,' he said, which caused an explosion of laughter from the other two because McMaster had failed to register Donohue's semi-audible contribution to the conversation.

I slammed my hopeless hand down on the table and took a sip of the rum that Bryant dispensed from his private store every evening.

'He's smart,' said McMaster. 'But not as smart as he thinks he is.'

'Is that what you think I am?' I said, not meaning to sound belligerent, except that I was on the way to getting drunk and must have raised my voice.

McMaster told me to calm down, then explained what he meant. 'Boys like you don't belong in the army because the guiding principle of the army is mateship and you're nobody's mate. I don't mean that as a criticism,' he said.

'You've hurt his feelings,' said Bryant.

He reached out and tried to slap me on the shoulder, but I ducked away just in time. I didn't like Bryant. I didn't like the way he was always trying to touch me. He'd grab hold of me when- ever I walked into a room and twist my arm up behind my back or grip my head in a headlock. I had to promise him something before he'd let me go, always the same thing. I had to agree to have sex with one of the Jap girls for free, as his gift to me for my eighteenth birthday. He'd arrange the whole thing, he said. *Do you promise?* he said. *Are you a boy or a man?* In front of a roomful of witnesses I had to swear to go through with it. And after I'd sworn on my mother's life, he'd release me and shove a couple of fags down my shirtfront to seal the deal.

He winked at me now and laid his cards down for McMaster and Donohue to see.

'Cunt,' said Donohue.

'Watch your language,' said Bryant. 'There are children present.'

He gathered up his winnings and waited for me to shuffle the pack and hand it back to McMaster so he could deal.

'Of course that's complete bullshit,' Donohue said to no one in particular. 'The guiding principle of the army is sexual deprivation. Lock a whole bunch of men up for weeks at a time with no women and of course the result is they want to kill people. It stands to reason.'

'You're such a crude bastard,' said McMaster. 'Not everything's about sex.'

'Yes it is,' said Donohue.

'You're very quiet,' said Bryant, turning his gaze in my direction. He smiled at me, showing a row of tobacco-stained teeth hanging loosely from the gums.

'I agree,' I said.

Bryant raised his eyebrows in mock surprise and turned to Donohue.

'He agrees,' he said.

Donohue extended his arm across the table and offered to shake my hand, but I declined. I looked straight at Bryant instead.

'You *are* a cunt,' I said.

Bryant chuckled to himself. Then he grabbed hold of the back of my neck before I could stop him.

'That's precisely what McMaster was talking about,' he said. 'That kind of lip is why you don't have any mates.'

I struggled to get loose from his grip.

'You gonna stick it in one of the Jap sheilas on your birthday like you promised?' he said.

I told him he better get me a pretty one and that made him laugh so much he let me go. For the rest of the game he kept pointing his finger at me like it was a gun and pretending to shoot.

I thought a lot about what Donohue had said about the army because it made me realise I wasn't alone in thinking about sex all the time. In my naivety back then I'd imagined that men grew less and less interested in sex the older they became. But Donohue and Bryant seemed just as preoccupied with their sexual fantasies as I was with mine. I didn't know what to make of this at first, whether to be disgusted and ashamed on their behalf, or whether to be relieved that I wasn't the only one. If anything, my experience with May had only made my condition worse, because it had been such a failure. The truth was that May didn't interest me in a physical sense, no matter how hard I tried to reform myself. Stanley, on the other hand, only had to appear in the mess hall, or out on the parade ground boundary where he and Sawada's boys did their morning sun worship, for me to feel faint.

He even came to me in dreams, the way he'd looked in the infirmary, with his hair neatly combed and his green-flecked eyes watching me deal cards in my amateurish way. He talked to me in my dreams. He told me how the art of walking a tightrope was to fix on a point straight ahead of you and forget everything else. *If you even think of falling then it's all over*, he said as he demonstrated. I woke up out of these dreams in a sweat because I couldn't stand to watch him setting out across space with nothing to help him stay up there except his faith in himself. He would take the first few steps, then stop while the rope sagged and rebounded under his weight, and then his foot would slip and that's when I knew he wasn't going to make it. I'd be racing to try to break his fall, or I'd be holding onto him afterwards, cradling his limp body in my arms and kissing him. Sometimes, if he was still conscious in the dream, and inclined to do so, he would kiss me back. Clearly the Akutagawa story he'd translated for me fed into these dreams. Stanley was the fictional thief who climbs towards paradise on a spider's thread. There were times when I dreamed I was waiting for him in the fragrant heavenly garden with the Buddha standing beside me.

When I woke up and found myself back in my bunk with the blanket half off and my backside hanging out in the cold I wanted to die. While McMaster snored in the next bunk I would get up to go and take a shower before anyone else was awake. Under the freezing water I would contemplate how sick I was, a pervert, just like my father had known all along.

There were other times I tried to cure myself using some of the magazines that Bryant was always hawking around, but it never worked—no more than lying in my bunk before dawn trying to conjure up a vision of May wearing only her underwear, or using my weekly telephone call to ring her up and whisper sweet nothings back and forth down the line. The next time I saw her I told her. I didn't mention Stanley. I just said I thought there was something not quite right about me.

'You'll get better with practice,' she said.

She was only half-joking. It was over a month since I'd seen her at the farm and I was awkward in her company. We were sitting in a booth down the back of a cafe in Shepparton eating corned beef sandwiches and drinking strong tea with a bit of rum in it that I'd brought along to help me talk.

'It's not funny,' I said.

She made an effort to look serious but it was obvious she had no idea what I was trying to tell her. Neither did I for that matter, not really. For instance, I still believed that my feelings for Stanley might be treatable.

'Maybe I should see a doctor,' I said.

'What are you talking about?'

'There might be something I can take.' I wanted to believe this. I was impressed by something I'd heard from the other guards about the Jap pearl divers. According to rumour they liked to insert pearls under the skin of their pricks. I never asked why they would do something that painful but, in my ignorance, I decided it was some sort of a remedy.

May took hold of my hand and squeezed it.

'I'll help you,' she said. 'You don't need a doctor.'

I hadn't expected her to be so willing to assist. I was a little disappointed because a part of me had wanted her to berate me, then abandon me to my fate. Instead she was offering to cure me.

'Why are you so good to me?' I said.

'Because I love you,' she said, gathering up my hands now and clutching them like they were hers to keep. Which only made me more miserable, because all I could think of was the way Stanley had gripped my hand in the infirmary. It was as if all of May's intimacies were only good for triggering memories of Stanley, and all of her declarations of love were only preludes to his declarations of love, even if these were purely imaginary.

I must have written Stanley about a dozen letters, then burned them as soon as I had signed them. I would go over to the schoolroom in the middle of the night and sit at one of the benches, scribbling on a sheet of school paper as if I was writing out lines as a punishment. *I want you. I've wanted you from the first moment I saw you. I want to kiss you. I want to kiss your beautiful mouth, and then your neck and then your ear and then your cock. I'm dying of desire for you.* I remember once I even decided that I should deliver one of these pitiful notes to Stanley in person so I could watch him read it before I set a match to it. But I only got as far as the gate to Compound C before I chickened out and retreated to the latrines. I made myself come over the page of filth I'd written, then tore it to pieces and threw the whole mess down the shithole.

After that I stopped writing letters and started writing bad poems instead, some of which I've kept. When I read them now I pity the boy who dreamed them up so ineptly and earnestly all those years ago. It reads like the worst schoolboy poetry, although occasionally there is a sentiment that stands out from the rest as if, just for a moment, something honest had silenced the sublime music with which I was trying to drown it out. *There are no gods,* wrote my seventeen-year-old self,

> *only suns and moons and stars without feeling,*
> *telling us nothing about themselves except revealing*
> *beauty to us on every day. In the mornings and at night,*
> *we see each miracle by their light:*
> *each flower, each bird, each hand, each eye*
> *each look, each touch, each truth, each lie.*

I can see what that boy was trying to do. He was trying to turn his lust into high-minded religious rapture, because that way it might be easier to bear.

10

It might have been that I was influenced at the time by Stanley's religious conversion. If I was on night duty I made a point of hanging around at the back of the parade ground to watch him and his little band perform their prayers. The ritual took only a few minutes but it was still impressive. Just before dawn they would march out in the dark behind Baba-san and stand along the fence in a row. At first light they would sit down on their knees in the dust and bow to the rising sun. When the sun was up they would stand and make a formal bow to their teacher, Baba-san, and to Sawada, their leader. All of this was done in silence and with a simple reverence that affected me, despite my misgivings about its object, which I understood to be the Emperor.

After the ceremony, the boys trained, starting with warm-up stretches and ending with sprint races up and down the eastern length of the perimeter fence. Again, this was all accomplished in silence, apart from a few ritual exchanges back and forth. Baba-san didn't run. He paced up and down with his felt hat pushed back off his forehead and his hands thrust in his coat pockets. If anything he resembled a horse-trainer watching his prize gallopers out on the track. Sometimes he noticed me watching the boys too, and he would wave and I would wave back, as if he and I were collaborators in the racing game. Stanley, on the other hand, made a point of refusing to look at me. He would only look at Sawada. He stuck by the other boy and did whatever he did. It was as if he wanted me to see how devoted he was to his new friend, and how useless to him I'd suddenly become.

As soon as they were finished their final run the boys lined up in front of Baba-san and bowed again, barking a rapid-fire call-and-response routine. Then they reverted from a disciplined squad into a rabble, all trying to trip each other up or ride piggyback as they made their way to their huts to shower and change for morning parade. I never watched them without a pang of jealousy, particularly Sawada, with whom Stanley jostled and joined arms as they walked along, sometimes sharing a cigarette, no doubt one of the Camels I'd given him.

Of course it puzzled me what Stanley or any of the others saw in Sawada. I'd only spoken to him once, when I was on escort duty, in charge of delivering him from the lock-up back to his compound. He was a thin, sallow boy with a face like a lizard and a head of wiry hair that grew straight out like bristles. When I asked him whether his mother had recovered from the chair-leg attack he ignored me.

'He's all yours,' I said to the compound leader. Maeda was one of the old men I'd seen holding court with Baba-san in the mess hall. He was slight and a full head shorter than me, but he managed to intimidate me by his stare alone. As soon as my back was turned Sawada said something in Japanese to Maeda that made him laugh. I turned around and found Sawada smiling at me. He still didn't say anything but his manner was so contemptuous it made me momentarily breathless.

Riley called him the Sorcerer's Apprentice, and told me that everything Sawada had learned he'd learned from Baba-san. 'And now he's got his hooks into Stanley,' he said. 'Which is a real shame.'

I said I thought it might be only temporary, that Stanley didn't strike me as a joiner. Of course I was echoing what McMaster had said about Stanley, and hoping that he was right.

'Any port in a storm,' said Riley.

This was over breakfast in the guards' mess one morning in the middle of July. McMaster and Riley had been discussing the situation in Burma—it seemed that the Japs were on the run, scrambling to get out by whatever means they could.

'Anybody want to bet it'll all be over before August?' said McMaster.

Nobody took him up on it. Bryant already had a book running on the exact day of the Jap surrender, but everyone had it falling sometime around December after the Yanks had firebombed every town and village in the country.

'Baba-san's not giving up yet,' said Riley. 'I see he's signing up some new storm-troopers.'

'Delusions of grandeur,' said McMaster.

I didn't really understand why Baba-san was allowed to reign over his boys the way he did, but then I hadn't been at Tatura long enough to understand its special pathology. Riley and McMaster both agreed that, as long as order was maintained, it was better to leave the internees to their own devices. If they were wrongheaded about the war then that wasn't really anyone else's problem but theirs, and anyway events would overtake them soon enough.

This insouciance about the Japs struck me as a brand of laziness, and it made me apprehensive to watch how the numbers at Sawada's table kept increasing. My main concern was for Stanley, because I didn't want him to get into any trouble. Within a few days of Stanley joining them, Sawada's gang had commandeered a second table in the mess and filled it with recent converts to the cause. Baba-san liked to go over and preach to them occasionally. He'd been a language professor it was said, and he spoke in a monotone, as if he was delivering an interminable seminar. The one thing he never did was to smile.

'He's telling them the emperor needs them for a sunbeam,' said Riley, pausing to watch them the next time we were on duty together.

I watched the way Stanley sat with his arms crossed and an expression of deep melancholy on his face. Whatever Baba-san was saying must have been upsetting, because all the boys looked equally downcast.

'More bad news,' said Riley.

'Either that or his jokes aren't very funny,' I said. It still struck me as absurd that Stanley had turned into one of these sorrowful boys, when I'd formed such a different impression of him. I was in no position to know what had triggered his transformation. All I had to go on was our conversation outside the back of the schoolroom when he'd mentioned his 'plan'. For all I knew he might have turned for no better reason than that he was easily bored and in need of some elaborate form of entertainment. Every time I saw him I looked for a sign that he was faking his conversion, playacting the role of religious disciple, but none was forthcoming.

Colonel Hollows must have sensed unrest brewing. He took to making speeches after morning roll call in which he advised everyone to keep calm. The war, he said, was coming to an end. The Americans had taken the fight right to the doorstep of the Japanese main islands. Thousands upon thousands of Japanese civilians had lost their lives in Okinawa, often at the hands of their own troops. Many thousands of Americans had also perished. The operations in Borneo and in Burma were designed to cut the enemy forces off from all remaining supply and command routes. Again and again, he told the internees that, although passions were bound to be running high, at this time the best course of action was to wait patiently for the inevitable end of hostilities and to refuse to react to rumour and speculation. He also warned that anyone who was found to be fanning unsubstantiated rumour, or to be plotting retribution in the camp, would be severely punished.

Pissing in the wind, McMaster called it. He didn't think Hollows had a hope of stopping the rumour mill at Tatura, or of preventing talk of vengeance. 'You might as well order them to stop breathing,' he said.

Once I was more relaxed around them, I asked the kids what they thought about the war. They said America would win, but when I asked what would become of them once that happened, they went quiet. A lot of them were too young to remember where they'd lived before the war and struggled when I asked them to describe what it was like at home.

'Do you want to go back there?' I said.

Opinion was divided. A majority of the older ones said yes, but the younger ones said no.

'Why not?' I said.

'I like it here,' they said, parroting each other.

'Why?' I said.

Some mentioned their friends and some said that their mothers wanted to stay because it was better than Japan.

'If we go back to Japan they'll kill us,' said one boy.

'Who told you that?' I said.

'My brother,' he said.

I knew his brother. He was one of Sawada's followers. I assumed this was something he'd heard from Baba-san or Maeda.

'Why would they kill you?' I wanted to know, because there was every reason to believe that it might be true.

The boy shifted in his seat and hesitated to answer. I told him it was all right if he didn't want to say anything, but then he suddenly stood up and started to speak very fast. It was as if this had been weighing on his mind for a long time, like an admission of guilt.

'Because it isn't right to be a prisoner. It's a duty to sacrifice your life for your country and for your emperor, and anyone who doesn't sacrifice his life is a traitor.'

The other kids glanced at each other and one or two giggled.

'Do you believe that?' I said.

When the boy didn't say anything I told him to sit down. I asked the others what they thought and some of them said they didn't agree.

'My mum says it's better to be a prisoner,' said a boy called Ralph Endo, who rarely uttered a word.

'Why does she think that?' I said.

'Because you get food and clothes for free,' he said. 'And you even get a doctor when you're sick or you're having a baby.'

Ralph's mother had had two babies in the time she'd been in Tatura and was pregnant with a third, even though Ralph's father was away at the single-men's camp. According to Riley, the father of Ralph's little half-sisters worked as a cook in the camp kitchens. His real name was Evans but the guards all called him Rabbit.

'What will you do when the war's finished?' one of the girls asked me. She was from New Caledonia and everyone knew her as the kid who'd deserted the Jap school because of a disagreement with Baba-san about the emperor's divine status. When she'd told Baba-san that she was a Catholic and believed in only one God, he'd slapped her so hard across the face that her cheek had split open. The scar was still visible.

I wasn't prepared for the question so I blushed and made up an answer.

'I'm thinking I might open a photography studio,' I said.

They knew I had a camera because they'd followed me around

one day while I took some shots of life around the camp. Another time I'd taken a group photo of them all lined up outside the schoolroom, as well as shots of a few of them on the tennis court with Stanley.

'What if Japan wins the war?' she said.

'I don't think that's very likely,' I said.

'Neither do I,' she said. But she looked worried anyway.

They all did, most of the time. I noticed how many of their games involved battles to the death. The boys enacted campaigns around the outside of the huts, involving pretend kamikaze missions and mass suicides. The girls took part as well, letting themselves be taken hostage and locked up in make-believe caves, then blown to bits with imaginary hand grenades they'd pretend to trigger on hearing that the Americans were coming to get them.

Disturbed by what he saw as an impending collapse in morale, McMaster came up with a plan to distract the kids from their grim preoccupations. Towards the end of July he decided to program an impromptu school concert. He put up posters all over the camp. Requests poured in from the parents wanting permission to help out. Stanley's uncles promised him a circus show, and a few musicians decided to play for the older kids so they could stay up late and dance after the concert was finished. The women volunteered to work in the kitchen for the night and give some of the cooks a day off. Apparently it was a tradition in Tatura to stage such entertainments—film nights, Japanese festivals, musical evenings. McMaster told me to be prepared. 'They're a real eye-opener,' he said.

Not everyone was as enthusiastic as he was about the Japs enjoying themselves in this way. A lot of the other men thought it was spoiling them. Bryant even suggested it was unpatriotic.

'That's a big word,' said McMaster. 'It's just a bit of fun.'

We were drinking together one frigid evening, trying our best to stay warm.

'I don't see the point,' said Bryant. 'It just gives them ideas.'

'Exactly,' said McMaster. 'It gives them something to think about other than their blighted lives. It shows off how much raw talent there is out there going to waste.'

There was a pause, during which I could see McMaster glancing at Bryant's cards.

'I reckon,' said Donohue, in a kind of reverent whisper. 'Speaking of talent, have you seen the pair on that Dutch sheila Sophie whatsername. She can't be more than twelve years old.'

'Eighteen,' said Bryant. 'I checked.'

'What do you do?' said Donohue. 'Just go up and ask them?'

'There's no law against it,' said Bryant.

'What if you get caught?' said Donohue.

'I don't know what you're talking about,' said Bryant. He smiled at me and took a swig of rum from the bottle. 'Do you know what he's talking about Artie?'

I told him my name was Arthur then laid down an unbeatable hand for him to inspect.

'Bugger me,' he said.

'Not if you paid me a million quid,' I said.

I let him slap me on the back and tug hard on my ear and then I told him to take his hands off me because I didn't think it was normal the way he kept wanting to touch me.

He pinched my cheek hard enough to make it sting. 'When's your birthday again?' he said. He knew very well when it was but he wanted me to tell him one more time in front of the others.

'August,' I said.

'What day in August?' he said.

'Seventeenth,' I said.

He tapped a finger on his right temple and told me he hadn't really forgotten. He had the date stored away in his brain he said, because it was so important.

'That wouldn't leave room for much else then,' said Donohue who was gathering up the cards and preparing to shuffle the pack again.

Bryant turned to him and smiled. 'Shame,' he said. 'I was going to offer you the lovely virgin with the big knockers. But I just changed me mind.'

'You're a complete degenerate,' said McMaster.

'I do believe you're jealous,' said Bryant, cackling in the way he liked to when he was pretending to enjoy himself.

'There are other things in life,' said McMaster, 'besides women and money and grog.'

'I'd like to know what they are,' said Bryant.

'Beauty,' said McMaster. 'Poetry. Great art. True love.'

'Stop,' said Bryant, 'before you make the kid cry.'

He turned to look at me, waiting for a reaction. I gathered up my winnings and rose from the table.

'Where are you going?' said Bryant.

'Over to the store,' I said, 'to put in a call to my girl.'

'She gonna give you one for your birthday too?' he said.

'Maybe,' I said.

'What a busy boy,' he said.

'I do believe you're jealous,' I said.

Bryant blew me a kiss. 'I don't mind sharing,' he said.

I called May as I'd promised to and thanked her for her last letter. She'd written to ask me what I wanted for my birthday.

'I'm surprised you remembered,' I said.

'Of course I remembered,' she said.

'It doesn't seem all that important,' I said.

'It is to me,' she said. 'I feel like you're catching up with me at last. We're practically grown-ups.'

I told her I missed her and that I would write again soon and she promised to write back.

'You didn't tell me what you wanted for your present,' she said.

'You know what I want,' I said, trying to sound sexy.

She giggled. 'I love you,' she said.

'I love you too,' I said. My voice sounded hollow down the phone, like it was echoing in a cave.

On my way back to the barracks I stopped in at the school-room and sat down at one of the benches to write one of my pathetic notes to Stanley but all I produced was *Dear Stanley, Fuck you, love Arthur.* I stared at what I'd written for a long time and then I took the piece of paper outside in the cold and set fire to it with the end of my cigarette. I remember the burning page breaking up as I waved it around, sending fragments up into the air where they melted away to nothing.

11

The concert was scheduled for the evening of August the tenth. I looked forward to it because the kids' excitement leading up to the event had infected even me. I also thought there might be an opportunity on the night for me to get Stanley on his own. In fact, for weeks on end, I thought about little else. At the same time I continued to correspond with May, lavishing on her all of the endearments that I dreamed of directing at Stanley once we were alone together. If May ever detected any insincerity, she never let on. It wasn't in her nature to be suspicious or mistrustful. That was one of the things that had attracted me to her in the first place.

Meanwhile Stanley, for his part, continued to ignore me. He and Sawada had become inseparable. When they weren't in Baba-san's schoolhouse helping to teach the younger children, they were hanging around outside in the cold talking with their inner circle and sharing smokes. Worse still, the two of them would often head off together on long walks around the perimeter fence, because this gave them a chance to talk in private. Riley called them Dr Jekyll and Mr Hyde and when I asked him which was which he said they were the same man, which was the whole point.

'Pardon my ignorance,' I said.

'Much learning doth make thee mad,' said Riley almost to himself.

He was standing guard with me at the end of an unscheduled evening roll call. In the morning we'd heard the news about the bomb dropped on Hiroshima. I don't claim I understood at the time how momentous an event this was. All I did know was that it was likely to bring the war to an end sooner rather than later. By then I had no doubt that the war was won; it was just a matter of when the Japs would decide to surrender. The point of the extra parade in the evening of that day had been unclear. Our only task seemed to be to keep watch while the internees milled about on the parade ground. They seemed more and more reluctant to break up and go indoors in case there was some detail they'd missed hearing, something decisive that would clarify what the news might mean for them. The men who'd been away gathering firewood in the bush that day, and the women who'd been at work in the clothing factory, all wanted to hang around asking questions and listening out for any scrap of information that was going the rounds. This was exactly the rumour-mongering Colonel Hollows had cautioned against, but he seemed to feel it was an understandable impulse under the circumstances.

I could just make out Stanley and Sawada in the distance. They were sitting on the steps of the Jap school, at a slight remove from the other boys in their group. I watched them lean their heads together as if everything they had to say was just between the two of them.

'I suppose Baba-san has told his boys that the Hiroshima story's all lies,' I said.

'No doubt,' said Riley. 'I find it hard to believe myself.'

We were yet to see the pictures in the newspaper, but we'd heard the descriptions of the new bomb's destructive power. It was said that sixty-five thousand people had died in Hiroshima in less than a second.

Riley and I continued to watch the crowd of inmates drifting around in the gathering dusk.

'Every morning they all get out of bed,' said Riley. 'They put on their clothes and get their kids washed and dressed and their hair brushed with little ribbons and such. Have you noticed how you rarely see a dirty kid?'

'Ralph Endo's a bit grubby,' I said, thinking of the mornings I'd taken Ralph round to the washbasins and given his face a good scrub before school. I could see him now in the distance piggy-backing one of his sisters round in circles while his mother stood gossiping, her belly ballooning out in front of her so far she had to lean backwards to stop herself from keeling over.

'It's a different kind of warfare,' said Riley, 'when you target women and children and old men just going about their daily business.'

'The Japs should have surrendered,' I snapped.

Riley glanced at me, clearly surprised by my vehemence.

'It's not how we fought the last war,' he said. 'Your enemy was the other soldier. It was kill or be killed.'

'They were warned,' I said.

'So that makes it all right does it?' said Riley.

'If it means we've won,' I said.

On the day before the concert news came through that a second atomic bomb had been dropped on Nagasaki, killing around forty thousand. By then I think everybody knew what was going to happen next. The Japs were going to finally accept what the rest of us already knew. Not that there was an immediate recognition at Tatura of the ramifications of defeat. We were a long way from the centre of things; the whole rationale of the camp had been to cut off all communications with the outside world. As a result, the dawn of the atomic age was experienced as an abstraction, or a dream, rather than as a fact.

The concert went ahead as planned. The girls all came in their best dresses, some of them in kimonos, with special white socks and wooden clogs. The boys came in ties and jackets, and the men in suits or kimonos their wives had stitched together out of whatever they could salvage in the factory. Only the Sawada boys hadn't bothered to dress up for the occasion, turning up in their usual black outfits, with their bare heads as pale as stones. I'd been right about Baba-san. One of the kids told me the old man had come round to his hut in the night to talk to his mother and his brothers and sisters. He'd instructed the whole family not to pay any heed to the rumours about a new kind of bomb, because they weren't true. There was no such thing.

I didn't get to see much of the concert in the end. I was on duty outside the mess hall, checking everyone who went in or out. All I could do was crane my neck to get a view of a narrow section of the stage to one side. The rest I had to imagine. Stanley hadn't arrived at the mess hall with Sawada so I guessed he must be appearing with the circus. I waited for a glimpse of him for over an hour and a half, right through the first half of the show and through the dinner break. It didn't seem fair that McMaster had got the night off to help the kids, while I had to stand outside in the freezing wind. After the break I watched the two kids on the end of the row, Billy and Rose Watanabe, brother and sister, belting out 'The Isle of Skye' and 'Pack up Your Troubles In Your Old Kit Bag'. I nearly cried with relief when the songs ended and the hall filled with applause. Next there was a sorrowful and unrelenting tune on the Japanese recorder, and after that a comic routine in Japanese by two teenage boys who hadn't rehearsed for long enough and kept forgetting their lines.

I caught sight of Stanley as he lined up with Shigeru and his other uncles at the bottom of the steps leading to the stage. Dressed in their colourful gowns, the men seemed to have undergone some miraculous transformation. It helps to remember that I'd so far been completely starved of entertainment at Tatura. The world of the camp was uniformly grey and drab, so the appearance of Stanley and the other acrobats in all their silk finery was like a vision. I watched entranced as they disrobed at the top of the stairs. Underneath their gowns they were wore nothing except plain white shorts, startling in their brevity. They may as well have been naked. Amidst applause and raucous laughter they started straight into their juggling act, using dinner plates at first and then incorporating fans and Japanese umbrellas. At the height of the act the stage was a flurry of flying objects all kept in motion at once. Stanley's hands moved so fast it was impossible to see them, but the rest of him was immobile, always in a state of readiness for the next thing. It was as if his breathing was suspended—along with my own—until the umbrellas and plates and fans had all come to a standstill.

Their second act was to build a tower out of chairs and balance on them. Stanley was the last to climb the tower and that was the only time I had an uninterrupted view of him. By then I'd pushed inside and climbed on a table up the back of the hall. At the top of the tower Stanley performed a handstand then started to descend the tower on his hands. About halfway down he launched himself into a somersault and landed squarely on his feet centrestage. I watched while Stanley took his bow. Then he disappeared down the steps, his silken gown draped over his shoulders like he was a boxer leaving the ring.

I hadn't expected to see anything so accomplished. I suppose I'd imagined a few tawdry tricks performed without much enthusiasm. Instead, the circus had dazzled everyone in the place. I realised the troupe must have been in constant training. I also understood Stanley's devotion to running. His body had changed in the last few weeks. He was no taller but he seemed to have grown in strength and stamina, with the result that his beauty was even more heartbreaking than before. I stood outside in the cold and tried to hold onto the vision of him balancing at the top of the human tower with his arms outstretched and a half-smile on his face. He had offered himself up to the audience almost spitefully. I thought I had never seen anyone so unhappy in all my life.

In retrospect it was no real surprise what happened next. Anyone paying attention would have sensed trouble brewing. It was like a gradual shift in the barometric pressure. I searched for Stanley in the crowd as the chairs were cleared out of the hall and the band set up for the dance. I was worried that he might have left before I had time to speak to him. As the dance got under way the Sawada boys glared from the sidelines. They waited for the first few bars of the opening number to finish then they muscled their way through the dancers and climbed onto the stage. I stood at the doorway and watched while a couple of them tried to manhandle the musicians off the stage. The audience shouted at them to stop and let the band keep playing. Then Baba-san appeared and mounted the stairs. Everyone went quiet as he started his sermon. He spoke in Japanese, while members of the crowd tried to drown him out in English, saying he was telling lies and trying to stir up trouble for no reason. When the old man could no longer be heard, Sawada started to yell at the top of his voice so everyone could hear.

'Why you dancing and singing?' he shouted. 'Japanese people die.'

It was more of a plea than anything else. You could tell the kid was hysterical. He kept wheeling around and pointing at the musicians. They'd fought off their attackers and were refusing to move.

'Why you play American music?'

'Because it's better than Jap music,' somebody in the crowd called out.

Sawada spun around again, searching wildly for whoever had spoken.

'You die,' he said. 'I kill you.'

By then Colonel Hollows had arrived on the scene, flanked by a few extra guards. First he ordered Baba-san off the stage, then he approached Sawada and the other boys and called them to order. They fell into line immediately and Hollows mounted the stage.

'The evening's entertainment is over,' he bellowed. 'You will return to your huts and prepare for lights out. There will be a special hut inspection at twenty-one hundred hours. Anyone not in their quarters at that time will be arrested and placed in the lock-up on half rations.'

The guards herded the boys out of the hall, Sawada bringing up the rear. He didn't go quietly. He kept shouting the Japanese battle cry, *Banzai! Banzai!* Some of the older men in the hall briefly took up the cry, but when the crowd told them to shut up, they shuffled out the doors with everybody else.

I took advantage of the general chaos to hurry over to Stanley's compound. I wanted to know why he'd left the dance early and deserted the other boys and I had to warn him about the hut inspection. I also had a short speech prepared about the bombing of Nagasaki. The crude triumphalism I heard every day from Bryant and some of the others had made me uncomfortable and I wanted Stanley to know that. In Bryant's opinion the Americans should just keep dropping A-bombs until every Jap city had been reduced to ashes. *Blast the whole fuckin' country back to the stone age,* he said. When someone pointed out that there were allied POWs in camps all over Japan, Bryant was unmoved. *You take your fuckin' chances when you sign up for this job,* he said.

I found Stanley standing under the light outside his hut, having a smoke. If he was surprised to see me he didn't show it, he just kept leaning against the wall and staring at his shoes.

'What happened to you?' I said. 'Why didn't you stay for the dance?'

'My mother's sick,' he said.

I could hear voices from inside the hut. I assumed it was his mother who was crying.

'I'm sorry,' I said.

Stanley didn't reply.

'Sawada's gone to the lock-up,' I said.

'Where he belongs,' said Stanley.

I couldn't tell whether he cared or not. I watched the way he dangled his cigarette out of the corner of his lips. I hadn't seen him do that before. I guessed it was another habit he'd picked up from his friend.

'There's a hut inspection at nine,' I said.

'I know.'

He still hadn't looked at me. He kept kicking the dirt with the toe of his shoe.

'They're saying the Japs will have to surrender now,' I said.

'Looks that way,' said Stanley.

'Should have given up weeks ago if you ask me. It would

have saved so many lives. It would have spared Hiroshima and Nagasaki.'

This brought a faintly mocking smile to Stanley's face.

'What's so funny?' I said. 'You think I'm wrong?'

Stanley finally looked up at me, still smiling.

'No,' he said. 'You're perfectly right.'

His mother continued to cry inside the hut behind us. Stanley didn't seem to be taking any notice of her, even though her cries sounded desperate.

'Is she okay?' I said.

He didn't answer. Instead, he walked around to the back of the hut, where the wailing was less audible, and I followed. As soon as I caught up with him he turned to me, took hold of my arm, and slid a small package into the pocket of my jacket.

'That's for Hollows,' he said. 'Don't show it to anyone but him.'

I went to take the package out of my pocket but he grabbed hold of my wrist.

'Leave it,' he said.

'Why? What's in it?'

'I've written you a letter,' he said. 'It explains everything.'

It was hard to make out his face in the darkness but I could hear him sniffing from the cold. Underneath his overcoat he was still wearing only his silk gown and his white shorts.

'What will I tell Hollows?' I said.

'Just tell him to read it.'

He finished his smoke and flicked the butt out into the blackness where it gave off a few sparks then dropped out of sight.

'Can I read it too?' I said.

'As long as you don't blab about it to everyone,' he said.

'I wouldn't do that,' I said.

'Make sure you don't,' he said.

After a pause he gave me a lopsided smile, as if he was embarrassed.

'Do you want me to suck your dick?' he said.

I knew he was trying to make fun of me.

'Jesus, Stanley,' I said. 'I've actually taken a risk by coming to see you. I'm not even supposed to be here.'

'Quieten down,' he said. 'You're shouting.' He stepped forward so he was right up close to me.

'What are you doing?' I said.

'Stop talking,' he said, and then he kissed me hard on the mouth.

'Don't,' I pleaded once he'd stopped kissing me. 'Please.'

He fell to his knees and unbuttoned my flies and the next thing I came in his hand so fast he didn't even have time to get a proper hold of me. I remember at that point I leaned down and hauled him to his feet and held onto him so tight he couldn't move.

'I'm sorry,' I said, burying my face in his neck. I was trying not to cry.

'It's okay,' he said.

'I couldn't help it,' I said. I wanted to say other things as well, like how my prick had been hard the whole time I was watching him on stage, and how I lay awake at nights remembering the way he'd looked when he was naked and Matron Conlon was washing him down. And I wanted to plead with him to give up Sawada because nothing good would come of it. I had to convince him that his only real friend in the world was me. But there wasn't any time, because as soon as he heard his mother calling him from inside the hut, Stanley was gone.

Two days later I went to see Matron Conlon about my weak ankle. I'd rolled it jumping down from the table on the night of the concert and it had been swollen ever since. She told me that Stanley's mother had swallowed a bottle of detergent on the night of the concert in the hope that it would kill her.

'Poor woman,' she said whispering and tapping her fingers on her temple. 'She's not the full shilling.'

'What's wrong with her?' I said.

Matron Conlon drew in a breath. 'It's four years,' she said. 'It takes its toll. She's not been right in the head since they got here.'

She pressed around the base of my ankle to see if there was anything broken.

'Are you looking after that lad of hers?' she said.

When I didn't respond she looked up at me. I must have been blushing because she put her hand up to my cheek in a motherly way.

'I'm doing my best,' I said, allowing her to stroke the side of my face the way she liked to. I didn't mind. It wasn't as if she meant any harm by it, not like Bryant.

'I wish I could save every last one of them,' she said. 'They're just kiddies.'

She gave me a dreamy smile and looked down at my ankle

again, pressing around the scar from my motorbike accident. 'It's a weakness,' she said. 'There's no cure for it.'

I wasn't sure whether she meant my ankle, or my other affliction.

'It isn't easy,' I said. That was the closest I ever came to confessing my real feelings for Stanley to anyone.

Matron Conlon put her fat finger to her lips and winked at me boozily. Then she laughed and told me she had a brother who was like me.

'He's in the priesthood,' she said. 'Best place for him.'

12

Stanley's secret report was fifty pages of tiny lead-pencil scrawl, written in a hand-made notebook the size of a cigarette pack. In a preamble he described in stilted half-sentences how he'd decided to spy on his fellow Japanese. A lot of them posed, in Stanley's words, *a danger to themselves and the other internees because of fanatical belief in the divine powers of Emperor Hirohito.* In the front of the notebook he had made a list of his targets in alphabetical order starting with Baba-san and ending with Sawada. He'd addressed the report to Colonel Hollows personally and marked it *Top Secret,* in a gesture that I couldn't help feeling was meant to be comical.

In fact the whole tone of the writing suggested to me that Stanley intended the report as a joke. He'd written out long conversations between Baba-san and Maeda and between members of the Sawada gang, to whom he gave code names like *The Fox* and *The Raccoon*, but the more I read the more convinced I was that he'd made up the dialogue himself in an attempt to shape it and make it more dramatic. For this reason I decided that even if it was half-true, the report was completely useless. I even wondered if the whole thing hadn't been designed as a slap in the face to Colonel Hollows, in which case it would be better not to pass it on to him at all. I knew the colonel more by reputation than by direct contact, but I'd been told he had an unpredictable temper and absolutely no sense of humour.

The letter Stanley had written to me was in the same tiny scrawl, although its tone was more sincere. At the top of the page he'd written *Destroy This After Read* and then he'd tried to explain the cause of his unusual behaviour over the previous few weeks.

I'm sorry if I was stranger to you, but I can't tell anyone, not even my family, about my secret mission. I never joked when I told you I wanted to be a spy, but unfortunately when I offer my idea to the colonel he turned me down flat. It wasn't very clever of him actually, because there are secrets in this camp that none of you chaps knows anything about. You are blind and deaf to the real life of the people in here, so you need to pay more attention. I have another thing to tell you. I'm going to break out of here soon. When I do I'm going back to America so I can study and become a successful man. So I hope you too will come and play tennis there. I look forward to seeing you become a champion. Good luck, your friend Stanley.

It affected me the same way each time I read it, especially

the part about Stanley's plan to go to America. I didn't know any more than he did what was going to happen to the Japs after the war, but I feared the worst. Given this I found Stanley's optimism about his future unbearable. At the same time I couldn't help but pray for a miracle, not just for him but for me as well. I tried not to think too much about my prospects once the war was over. The photography studio wasn't realistic because I had no money and no track record. And my old dream of playing professional tennis was equally unlikely. Stanley's belief in me was so touching that, instead of destroying his letter the way he'd instructed me to, I wrapped it around the notebook and kept the package hidden in a drawer in the schoolroom that nobody ever opened.

I didn't write back to him. I was afraid to. I persuaded myself we'd have other chances to meet now that Sawada was locked away. I assumed, I suppose, that Stanley would seek me out in order to let the general populace see I was in favour again, and that all I had to do was wait for him to appear at the schoolroom the way he had before. I even hoped that our daily tennis matches would resume, because I longed to have the pleasure again of watching him through the schoolroom window. In the meantime I continued to pour my desires into poetry whenever I had the chance. McMaster had read a few of my earlier efforts and, as editor of the camp magazine, he'd encouraged me to submit some poems. I don't have any of these late epics in my possession now but I remember they were mainly about universal brotherhood and love, two of the schoolmaster's favourite topics.

McMaster was very complimentary. He was an enthusiastic contributor to the magazine himself. He wrote comic-strips mostly, for the amusement of younger readers. Bryant was his harshest critic, particularly if the butt of the comic-strip joke was a big, burly guard like himself, as it often was.

'Don't you think your eagerness to crawl up the collective arse of the Japs is a little excessive?' said Bryant. He was unpacking the fags and stockings he'd just picked up in town from his supplier.

'No more than your devotion to robbing them blind,' said McMaster.

Bryant peered at us through the sheer stockings and smiled.

'Simple supply and demand,' he said. 'The poetry of the marketplace.'

He grabbed hold of my copy of the latest *Tatura Tatler* and before I could stop him he started reading my contribution out loud.

I dreamed of a world of brothers;
A country where no borders divide man from man,
woman from child, husband from wife.

'Give it back to him,' said McMaster, seeing how impotent I was to stop Bryant. He was at least a foot taller than me and held the magazine above his head where I had no chance of reaching it.

'What are you?' he said. 'A fucking commo?'

'Give it back to him,' McMaster said again, this time as a threat.

Bryant threw the magazine over my head, too high for me to catch, and it landed a few feet away, near McMaster, who picked it up and handed it to me.

'You can't touch me,' said Bryant, glaring first at McMaster then at me. 'None of youse can touch me.'

'One of these days,' said McMaster. 'It's only a matter of time before you get what's coming to you.'

Bryant laughed with his tongue sticking out like a dog's, then he put the stockings right up to his nose and sniffed the scent of them.

'Don't I fuckin' know it,' he said.

Three days later the war officially ended. The first I heard of it was at morning roll call when Colonel Hollows got up on a special podium to make the announcement. The way he worded the news was confusing. He said that Japan had officially accepted the terms of the Potsdam Declaration and agreed to an unconditional surrender. He then paused and cleared his throat as if overcome with emotion. Following a moment of uncomfortable silence he pocketed his notes, tapped the microphone a couple of times then spoke into it haltingly.

'I know how many of you have waited for this day with a sense of disbelief and dread,' he said. 'To those people I give my word that no recriminations or acts of vengeance against you will be tolerated. This war has raged across the world for too many years already. It has taken the lives of too many innocent people. Let us not allow this spirit of violent hatred and fanatical destructiveness to dictate our behaviour here in this place at this time. Instead let us begin today the long process of returning the world to peace and civility.

'To those of you who, like me, have looked forward to this day with a sense of relief and deep sorrow I plead with you to act generously and in a spirit of reconciliation. Nothing can be achieved in the weeks and months ahead unless we decide to put aside our differences and embrace each other as fellow human beings, regardless of race or creed or religion. I firmly believe that this is the only way forward for all of us here, and indeed for the entire world.'

When he stopped speaking there was a silence unlike any I had ever experienced before. It was as if the air around us had suddenly thinned, and we were floating. Apart from the wail of a baby there wasn't a single human sound. The silence went on for so long and was so intense I wondered whether anyone had understood the meaning of the speech. Colonel Hollows must have had similar doubts because he tapped the microphone a second time before leaning into it and shouting.

'The war is over. We have won a great victory.'

In an instant explosion of joy Riley danced around me, kicking up the dust with his boots and making wild noises. He grabbed hold of me and made me dance with him and then we embraced and fell over together.

We weren't the only ones making fools of ourselves. A few of the women were wheeling each other around and crying while their kids stood by and watched, confused about whether to try to comfort them or not. When I got to my feet I looked for Stanley in the crowd and saw him propping up his mother who leaned into him as if she might be about to faint. His uncle Shigeru and the rest of the family were standing in a line, shoulder to shoulder, their arms around each other. They were all laughing and crying at the same time.

Up on the podium Colonel Hollows was waiting now for a radio operator to set up the microphone so it could pick up a special recorded broadcast of the emperor announcing the surrender. At a sign from the operator, Hollows called for everyone to pay attention again and remain silent if they wanted to hear the emperor's words for themselves. What followed was as confusing for those of us who understood no Japanese as Hollows' speech must have been for those who didn't understand English. The emperor spoke in a strange, high-pitched monotone, like a nervous girl. I watched the faces in the crowd for some sign of a reaction, but there was none, only universal puzzlement. At the end of the speech there was another long silence, then the sound of sobbing drifted across the parade ground as numbers of men and women broke down.

Baba-san was one of them, so was Maeda. A while later, after everyone else had drifted away and gone back to their huts, the two old men were still sitting on their haunches in the dust, refusing to move. When Sturgess, one of the gunners, yelled at them from the watchtower to follow orders and return to their compound, they ignored him. Eventually it was Stanley who intervened. He stood between them and the watchtower and told Sturgess to please lower his rifle. Then Stanley turned to the old men and bowed. Whatever he said next it worked. They stood up and dusted themselves off and allowed Stanley to lead them away to their quarters.

Later I heard from Riley that Stanley had volunteered to go to the cells with a few of Baba-san's boys, to tell Sawada that the war had ended. Sawada had apparently shown no emotion, but the others had cried like babies and could not be persuaded to stop. The next time I saw them as a group was about a week later, after their leader had been released. They were all standing around waiting to see Sawada loaded onto a lorry with his belongings. They had abandoned their black uniforms and lost a lot of their insolence, even if a few of them still had the same joyless countenance as before. As soon as their friend appeared, flanked by two transport guards, they all bowed, Stanley included. Then they lined up along the inside fence. I was on the outside where the truck was waiting. Sawada glanced at me as he passed, his lizard eyes as expressionless as ever. Even so I experienced a pang of sorrow at the sight of him. He was pale and undernourished from refusing to eat and his shaved head was blue from the cold. He was technically too young to be going to the single-men's camp but his record of defiance and rebelliousness had weighed against him and Hollows had sought special permission to have him moved.

His mother was standing at the fence too, alongside the boys. She was a tiny woman, already grey-haired and hunched although she couldn't have been more than forty years old. When the truck drove off with her son in the back of it she called out his name over and over again, and then she trotted along, crying and calling out, until she reached the corner of the fence and could go no further. A few moments later the lorry reached a bend in the road and disappeared in a cloud of powdery dust, leaving her standing there all alone. I watched her fall to her knees and beat on the ground with her fists.

The boys were crying too, but silently, all except Stanley. He was dry-eyed and smoking a fag in the way he liked to now,

135

dangling it from the corner of his mouth. I think he thought it made him look tough, but every time I saw him do it I wanted to laugh because this gesture, like all of the others he practised, was an act. I knew that because I tried the same tricks myself, in order to seem tougher than I was. Before he left that day he approached the inside fence and waved to me across the twenty yards or so that divided us.

'You still giving tennis lessons?' he called out.

I waved back and told him to drop round to the schoolroom whenever he felt like it. 'Maybe you could coach me,' I said. Then I told him to step back or I would have to wake up the gunner.

Stanley did as he was told, and when he was a good fifty feet away he shouted out.

'Is that far enough?'

'That's fine,' I said.

'Shoulders back,' he said, mocking my habitual slouch. He wanted to draw attention to me to entertain the other boys. He didn't mean any harm, I could see that, but I was still hurt by how he could switch from being someone who had made me come in his hand to being someone who mocked me in public. Again I understood that this was part of his survival strategy, but it confused me nonetheless. The next minute he was telling the boys he was getting together a baseball team to take on the Formosans and he was going to call it The Yankees, after the greatest baseball team in the world.

'Anybody want to come over to the winning side?' he said.

None of the boys wanted to. I could tell by the way they were glancing at each other as if they were ashamed. Then one of them said something in Japanese and started to walk away and the others followed him. Stanley trailed along after them, one of the group, but unlike them in every way. As if to emphasise the point he turned back after he'd gone a few paces and gave me a stiff salute. It made me think of a sailor on the deck of a sinking ship.

13

I'd telephoned May as soon as I could after the news of the surrender, expecting to find her still at the farm, but the farmer's wife said she had gone home to Melbourne. A couple of days later I received a parcel from her with a note saying she'd tried to call me but hadn't been able to get through.

I'm sorry, but I can't come to the victory dance with you. I'm staying at home in case we get some news about Owen. I hope you have a very happy birthday. Please wear this and think of me.
All my love my darling, xxxx May.

She'd also included a black and white photograph of herself and on the back she'd written *Me in my new dress. It's baby blue, the same colour as your beautiful eyes.* The dress had a high waist and a full skirt that came down to the calf. In it May looked full-figured and somewhat old-fashioned, like Little Miss Muffet, or Cinderella before the ball. I kept the photograph under my pillow along with her previous letters, but I never looked at it. And I never wore the tie she'd sent for my birthday either, even though it was silk and obviously expensive, because I decided that after what Stanley had done to me at the back of his hut, I didn't deserve to own it. That night, after I'd received the parcel, I sat in the schoolroom and wrote May a letter. I thanked her for the present and then I said I thought it would be better if we didn't see each other again. I was drunk at the time, as I was most nights by then, but I still had the presence of mind to burn the letter afterwards in the rubbish bin and scatter the ashes at the bottom of the steps, making sure to stamp them into the dirt with my boots before I left.

The dance was the day after my birthday. Under the circumstances I was glad to be going without May. It meant I could get loaded with Donohue and Bryant and the others before we left, and not have to worry about anything that happened after that. I can't remember how it was that we all got permission to be out all night, but I think it was one of the rare occasions when Hollows arranged a group of trusties to act as guards for the night.

Also I forget how I ended up with a woman called Hanako, out in the shed at the back of the kitchens at the Rushworth School of Arts. I refused to touch her even though Bryant had paid her to fuck me. I think she must have been one of the cooks who'd volunteered to prepare a supper for the victory dance. I only knew her by sight. She was older than me, probably twenty-five, and she had a daughter who'd been born in the camp a few weeks after Pearl Harbor. The daughter sometimes came to the school-room with a group of older girls and she'd sit quietly drawing or pretending to read while the older girls did their lessons. Her name was Junko and she had a face as round and pale as a moon. The fact that I knew the little girl made it hard for me to even look at her mother.

'You don't like me?' she said.

'No,' I said. 'I like you.'

Actually I hated her, I especially hated the effort she'd made to do her hair up and paint her lips. And I hated the way her skin glowed pink from standing over the steaming sink washing all the pots and pans.

'Maybe we can just talk,' I said, gesturing to her to do up the buttons on her blouse. 'I need to sit down.'

We were inside the shed. There was a long box up against the wall where I took a seat and motioned for her to come and sit next to me. I told her there was nothing to be afraid of because I wasn't going to say anything to Bryant, so she would get her money anyway and she could just say that I had a great time.

'And I'll tell him myself,' I said. 'I'll say it was the best birthday present anyone ever gave me.'

Hanako did up her buttons and put on her cardigan. It was cold in the shed but we had to stay there because Bryant had someone outside watching the door ready to yell out when we were finished.

'He say thirty minutes,' said Hanako.

'Mean bastard,' I said. I meant it as a joke but I don't think Hanako thought it was funny.

I asked her about her family and she told me her father was a laundryman from Neutral Bay in Sydney. He'd been there since 1934 until the day after Pearl Harbor when the police had turned up to tell them to pack a suitcase.

'They very nice,' she said. 'They searched the shop and the flat but they very polite. They said how sorry because I'm pregnant.'

She made a gesture to show me how big she'd been at the time and that's when I remember throwing up all over my boots. Hanako didn't know what to do at first but then she took off her apron and handed it to me so I could wipe my mouth on it and blow my nose.

'Sorry,' I said. 'It wasn't the food. Actually I didn't eat anything.'

'That's why you sick,' she said. 'Because you only drink.'

I stood up and tried to find some way to clean up the mess I'd made on the ground and on my boots. There was a hessian sack hanging from a nail on the wall so I took that down and spread it over the patch of sick. Hanako offered me a dishcloth to wipe my boots.

'I can wash later,' she said.

I thanked her and wiped my boots, then I rolled up the dishcloth and her apron in a tight ball and placed them next to her on the long box.

'He doesn't pay money,' said Hanako after a long pause.

'What do you mean?' I said, standing in front of her. I knew she must have been talking about Bryant but I couldn't understand what she was doing here if she wasn't getting paid.

'He promise to take me to Sydney,' she said. 'My father too.'

I still didn't understand. I asked her what exactly Bryant had told her he would do and she said there were other women as well who all wanted to stay in Australia now that the war was over.

'We want to go back to our houses,' she said. 'He can get us papers.'

I sat down next to her again but I couldn't think of anything to say because I couldn't be sure that what Bryant had told her was a lie. Maybe it was true. Maybe he could get them papers. Maybe he knew something none of the rest of us knew.

'You should be prepared,' I said. 'In case it turns out he can't help you.'

Hanako stared at me in the dark and smiled.

'What choice I have?' she said.

'I just think you should be careful who you trust,' I said.

She thanked me then leaned over and kissed me on the cheek. 'You a nice boy.'

When she said that I put my arms around her and clung to her for a few minutes to stop myself from crying, and also because it was so cold. After that I left the shed and went to take a piss in the bush. I must have seen our truck parked on the road on my way back to the hall and crawled into it to go to sleep, because that's where they found me when we left to drive back to Tatura at four-thirty in the morning.

'How's the birthday boy?' said Donohue, shaking me awake.

I couldn't talk. I just lay there under the tarpaulin and stared up at the stars.

Bryant came and leaned his face into mine, his breath stinking of cigarettes and grog.

'You didn't say thank you,' he said.

I stared at him and didn't say a word. He wore a triumphant expression that made me want to hit him, but in the end I reached both my arms out from underneath the tarpaulin and wrapped them around his neck, pulling him down so that I could kiss him on the mouth. Taken completely by surprise, he fell towards me and I clung even tighter to him, kissing him over and over again and thanking him, while the others screamed with laughter.

'Who said I don't have any mates,' I said. 'You're my mate. Thank you so much. She was the best fucking root. Like a bloody animal. Thank you and thank you again.'

Eventually Bryant got free of me and managed to sit himself back up on his seat.

'Yeah well,' he said. 'Just so long as you're grateful.'

'I'm so grateful I could suck you off,' I said.

Riley, in the driver's seat, cackled with laughter.

'You sick bastard,' said Bryant.

'You might like it,' I said.

After that everyone went quiet and then Donohue started to sing. *One day he'll come along, the man I love. And he'll be big and strong, the man I love.* I don't even think it was directed at Bryant but he suddenly leapt at Donohue and grabbed him round the throat.

'Shut the fuck up!' he screamed.

Riley slammed on the brakes to stop the truck, sending all of us tumbling forward and giving Donohue a chance to get free.

'The thing to remember,' said Riley, turning around to face us, 'is that in a few short weeks we'll all be walking out of Tatura camp for the last time and there's no way any of us is ever coming back.'

'Meaning what?' said Donohue.

Riley didn't answer for a moment.

'Meaning nothing at all,' he said eventually. 'It was just an observation.'

'Amen to that,' said Bryant, who hadn't exactly cheered up but was back in his seat and smoking contentedly. 'Can't come quick enough as far as I'm concerned.'

Except that even from where I was lying on the floor I could tell he didn't really mean it—he would miss the camp the way some people miss home.

It was dawn when we pulled up at the gates. We scrambled off the truck and filed past the guardhouse just as the sun was coming up over the low hills to the east, turning them pink. After what Riley had said on the road, and because I was still deranged with drink, I suddenly had the feeling I was seeing everything for the last time: fence, watchtower, parade ground, mess hall, all at the point of vanishing. And in that instant I completely forgot my hatred of the place, and my fear of the Japs and my unremitting desire for Stanley, and felt instead a wave of love so powerful I thought I would fall down from the force of it. I must have stopped walking and leaned dangerously because Riley waited behind and helped me to stand up straight.

'War is hell,' he told me.

I put my arm around his shoulder and leaned into him as if I was mortally wounded.

As soon as we were on the other side of the fence we sensed that some catastrophe had taken place in our absence. Even at that hour there should have been activity around the latrines and the showers, but the place was deserted. We crossed a silent parade ground and arrived back at our quarters where McMaster was waiting to relay orders. There'd been an incident, he said. We were all to report to Compound D immediately. If we needed to piss, like I did, that was too bad. McMaster didn't know the details any more than we did because he'd only just woken up himself. All he'd heard was that Baba-san was dead.

Once we'd made our way to the Compound D schoolroom, we discovered that Baba-san's wife had found him in the night. He'd hung himself from the rafters, with a suicide note and a photograph of the emperor in his breast pocket. He'd used strips of grey blanket knotted together for a rope. Nobody had thought to untie it and take it down along with the body, so the rope was one of the things you kept looking at, almost as if you were admiring his workmanship.

The other thing that made you morbidly curious was the body. It was laid on top of a row of stools pushed together to form a bench. I'd never seen a corpse. I waited until everyone else had taken a good look and then I approached, feeling a strange excitement. Baba-san's eyes were narrowly open beneath the lids. I have since seen the Buddha depicted with his eyes barely open, so detached from the world's suffering that he resembles a dead man. Baba-san's expression was the same, neither calm nor anguished, but something in between, the expression of someone who is beyond caring.

It was now a matter of keeping the news quiet until roll call so that Hollows could decide how much he was going to make of the incident, if anything. There was no chance of covering it up. Baba-san was one of the compound leaders. A lot of the Japs had looked to him for help and guidance over the years, and because his wife had found him and seen the truth for herself, there was no chance of passing his death off as a natural one. No doubt Baba-san had thought of all of this when he'd planned his departure. He'd even had the foresight to drape a hand-sewn Jap flag around himself so that his self-destruction could not be mistaken for anything merely personal.

A few days later Stanley came looking for me, as I'd hoped he would. I was spreading water on the vegetable patch behind the classroom, observed by an old man who came occasionally to give me advice about the garden. Mr Nakadai rested on the schoolroom steps and smoked one of my cigarettes. I glanced up from emptying a bucket of water over the cabbages and found Stanley standing right in front of me, dressed in an approximation of a baseball uniform. He'd even managed to procure a baseball cap from somewhere. I had a sudden desire to grab it off his head and make him wrestle me to get it back, and might have done so if Mr Nakadai hadn't been watching us so keenly.

'Were you there when they found Baba-san?' said Stanley.

'No,' I said. 'I came a bit later.'

Baba-san's death had not been broadcast in the end, but Stanley had obviously heard all the rumours.

I handed him a spare bucket and pointed to the tap.

'Was it suicide?' he said.

'I'd say so,' I said. 'There was a note.'

He went across and filled up the bucket then came back.

'What did it say?' he asked. I couldn't tell if he was just

curious, or whether Baba-san's death had affected him more deeply than he was letting on.

'No idea,' I said. 'Colonel Hollows took it. Closed the school down too.'

'I heard,' he said. 'What did they do with the body?' He crouched beside the leeks and started to splash water from his bucket around their roots.

'Buried it,' I said. I knew this because Donohue had been in the burial party. 'In the field behind the infirmary.'

'No funeral then,' said Stanley.

'No funeral,' I said.

Stanley stood up straight and emptied his bucket on some broccoli plants, spilling half of it on his new trousers.

'Don't spoil your uniform,' I said.

He ignored me and put his empty bucket down. I watched him bend forward to examine the leaves on the broad beans for slugs.

'What's the point of hanging yourself when the war's finished?' I said.

'If Japan lost we were all supposed to die together,' said Stanley. 'It was in my report.'

He looked up at me, disappointed that I didn't know this already.

'I must have missed that bit,' I said.

Stanley watched me cross to the tap and refill my bucket.

'Did you give my report to Hollows?' he said.

'Not yet,' I said.

'Why not?' he said.

I didn't answer straight away. I didn't want to offend him.

'Do you want it back?' I said. 'You can give it to the colonel yourself.'

'No,' he said. 'You keep it. Something to remember me by.'

He took out a folded sheet of paper from his trouser pocket.

'I wrote you another story,' he said.

He held the paper out to me. Mr Nakadai was up on his feet again and had resumed his inspection of the compost piles. He'd directed me to turn them once I'd finished watering.

'Thanks,' I said. 'I enjoyed the last one.'

Stanley bowed to me, then to Mr Nakadai. Without another word he marched off in the direction of the mess hall. After a few paces he started to rotate his arms as if he was trying to loosen his shoulders, then he held up an imaginary baseball bat and took a few swings at an imaginary ball. I assumed it was for my benefit, to make it seem like he was unmoved by what had happened to Baba-san, although even I could tell what a blow the old man's death had been, not just to Stanley but to everyone in the camp. It was as if it had made the defeat of Japan real and final. To those who'd never once entertained the prospect that Japan might lose the war, it must have seemed like the death of hope itself.

I wanted to go after Stanley and give him the smokes I had on me, but McMaster had his head out the schoolroom window and was calling me to come inside.

The story Stanley gave me was very short and read like a fairy tale. He'd illustrated it along the side of the page, just as he'd done with the story of the spider thread. I read it later by torchlight in my bunk, after everyone had gone to sleep. It was about a young painter apprenticed to a master who grew jealous of the young man's amazing skill. The master criticised the student constantly in front of the other apprentices until the young man despaired. Then one day the master told the student to paint a picture of a carp, and the student called to mind the fattest carp in his uncle's pond and painted it as best he could from memory. Furious at the boy's precocious talent, the master grabbed the painting and threw it into the water, where, to everyone's astonishment, the carp came to life and swam away. On the back of the story Stanley had written a woman's name, *Lily Tanaka*, and an address in Chicago.

Stanley had talked about escaping before, most recently in his secret letter, but I hadn't taken him seriously. It was always hard to tell whether he was showing off or not. Looking back I should have known that the story of the carp contained a message, that Stanley was saying his goodbyes. The address in America was the strongest clue, but even that I failed to pick up on, no doubt because I didn't want to.

Escape was a serious business. As far as I knew none of the Japs had ever tried it, let alone succeeded. Stanley, I suppose, had it in mind to show everyone how easily it could be done, if only you had the brains. In this sense his escape bid was more about his vanity than about his dream to reach Chicago. Not that I knew this at the time. Back then I thought Stanley must have lost his sanity. I blamed Baba-san. He'd deliberately set a precedent for boys of Stanley's temperament to follow, made it plain how much was at stake. For three days after Stanley went missing I survived on almost no sleep. I tossed and turned all through the night, fretting about whether he was dead in a ditch somewhere, either by his own hand or someone else's. My stomach pains and headaches came back.

When McMaster asked me what the matter was I told him it was my nerves playing up again. 'Matron Conlon says I need to learn to relax.'

'Quite right,' he said. 'You're too young to be rotting away in a place like this. Young fellow like you should be out dancing every night, meeting girls.'

I thanked him for the advice and tried to finish my morning toast, except that it tasted vaguely metallic and I ended up leaving most of it untouched.

I wrote Stanley a letter in the schoolroom late that night telling him to contact me as soon as he could.

Please let me know you're still alive. A postcard will do. Just a sign that you made it. I love you always, Arthur.

I read the letter again and again, delaying the moment when I would have to burn it. Before I left the schoolroom to go back to barracks I took Stanley's secret notebook out of the drawer where I'd hidden it and slipped it into the inside pocket of my overcoat. It was, as Stanley had said himself, something to remember him by. More than that, if Stanley was going to die I wanted to gather everything I could of his together. I imagined that this was somehow the solemn duty of the one who is left behind.

14

At the end of the week I watched, along with most of the camp, while Stanley was brought back in handcuffs by a couple of local policemen. It was mid-afternoon. Stanley had been on the loose since the Tuesday night when he'd dug his way out under the wire in the northern corner of the perimeter fence, near the tennis court. It seemed there was a depression in the ground there that had gone unnoticed and Stanley had only needed three or four hours to dig it out as he went, using a kitchen frypan he'd modified to function as a shovel. There was no suggestion that he'd any accomplices or any assistance from anyone inside or outside the camp. Nevertheless, Hollows was very careful to interview all the members of his family and all of the kids from the Jap school with whom Stanley had associated.

The guard on duty at the lock-up told me Stanley had been

picked up at Shepparton railway station, trying to board a moving freight train at eight o'clock in the morning. Apparently he'd lost his footing and fallen in the attempt and that's when he was spotted by the stationmaster, who detained him until the police arrived.

'Is he all right?' I asked.

'He'll survive.'

The guard's name was Perkins. He was a paunchy, balding, milky-eyed man with a reputation as a heavy drinker. That described almost everyone in the Tatura camp, but in Perkins's case drinking was as natural as breathing. He was like Matron Conlon, never truly drunk but never sober either. And like her he was everyone's friend, particularly if you were in the position to offer him some enticement. When I called in at the lock-up to see him he told me Stanley was in solitary for at least three weeks for what he'd done.

'Poor bugger nearly got away with it,' he said.

I took out a bottle of Bryant's rum with only an inch missing and offered it to Perkins.

'I'd like to see him,' I said. 'I want to ask him a few questions.'

'What for?' he said, eyeing the bottle.

'Curiosity,' I said.

'It's not allowed,' he said.

'Nor is drinking on duty,' I said. I gave the rum a shake so he could hear the sound of it slopping around in the bottle.

Perkins reached out his sizeable arm and wrapped it around my shoulder. 'Enough said.'

When I showed up at the cells that night Stanley seemed

unsurprised. He didn't even acknowledge me to begin with. It was only after I'd handed him a packet of smokes through the bars and helped him to light one that he eventually started to talk.

'What are you doing here?' he said, sounding bitter.

'I'll go if you don't want to see me,' I said.

He turned away and kept staring at the tip of his fag as if it held some mystery for him.

'You okay?' I said.

He showed me the raw patches on his knees where he'd lost some skin.

'What was the big idea?' I said.

It was a while before he answered and then it was in a low voice as if he thought there might be someone listening.

'No big idea,' he said. 'I just can't stand the pointless waiting around.'

I told him I understood, but he looked at me coldly and said nobody like me could possibly have the first idea what he was talking about.

'Why not?' I said.

'The minute I got to town it was all over,' he said. 'I should never have gone to town.'

'But you knew that before.'

'I forgot.'

He didn't sound sorry for himself, just angry. I wanted to reach through the bars and take hold of his hand but I was scared that Perkins might come in.

'Who's Lily Tanaka?' I said.

'My cousin.'

'How were you planning to get to Chicago?'

'Run.'

'How were you going to cross the Pacific?'

'Swim.'

I visited Stanley a few more nights after that, whenever Perkins was on duty. All the money I won at poker I spent on rum and Camel cigarettes. When Bryant noticed how much I appeared to be drinking and smoking I told him it was for health reasons.

'Doctor's orders,' I said.

I could tell he didn't believe me, but it didn't stop him selling me the stuff.

That same day I'd had a letter from May telling me the real reason she'd left the farm in such a hurry.

I'm three months pregnant. I should have told you before now, but I was too scared.

Numb with shock and apprehension, I'd been carrying the note around all day in the same pocket where I kept Stanley's report, as if the one had the power to cancel out the other.

'What are you doing after the war?' Bryant asked me.

'I've got no idea,' I said.

'I could use a bloke like you,' he said. 'Someone I can train up in the business.'

'Don't listen to him,' said McMaster.

I thanked Bryant and took the cigarettes and the two bottles of rum I'd paid for.

'You've got an honest face,' said Bryant. 'That's an asset in any game.'

I told Bryant that was the nicest thing he'd ever said to me and that I'd keep his offer in mind. And then I went outside to have a smoke and a quiet drink in private, except that McMaster came out to join me. He'd taken to mothering me since my recent bout of poor health.

'You all right?' he said.

'Fine.'

'You don't look fine. You look like you're carrying the weight of the world on your shoulders.'

I took out the envelope containing May's letter and handed it to him.

'What's this?' said McMaster. 'A Dear John letter?'

'Read it.'

McMaster opened the envelope. The letter was on mono-grammed paper and smelled of roses. When he'd finished reading he folded it and handed it back to me. I slid it back into my coat pocket.

'Christ,' said McMaster. 'That was fast work.'

'I don't know what to do,' I said.

McMaster patted my hand a couple of times. 'I have a joke for you,' he said. 'Do you know why the Labobo tribe in Africa discourage the young people from having sex?'

I shook my head.

'Because it might lead to dancing,' he said.

I smiled and then he gave me a stinging slap on the back and told me he wanted to be in the room when I broke the news to Bryant, because Bryant and the others had me down for a poof.

'We only did it the once,' I said, my smile vanishing. I don't know why I told him that. It sounded like I was trying to prove my innocence.

'What's that supposed to mean?' said McMaster, staring at me in an amused way.

'Nothing,' I said. 'Just that it seems like pretty bad luck.'

'I wouldn't say that to the girl if I was you,' said McMaster.

I offered him a swig of rum and he took it.

'You never know,' he said. 'It might be the making of you.'

I told Stanley about the letter the next time I saw him.

'I don't believe you,' he said.

'Believe what you like,' I said. 'I'm going down to Melbourne in the morning to see her. Three days compassionate leave.'

Stanley lit a smoke and took a long drag on it. He looked at me with his eyes narrowed, like he was a detective and I was a suspect.

'What was it like?' he said.

'Terrible,' I said. 'I was so nervous.'

'I've never been with a girl,' he said. 'Never even come close.'

'Maybe you should,' I said.

'Maybe,' he said.

He gave me a toothy smile. 'I could have any girl I wanted,' he said. 'They're hanging around outside my door every night of the goddamned week.' He made it sound as if the girls should have known better.

'It's because of the way you juggle,' I said. All I could think about was how it would feel to kiss him properly on the mouth.

'That's what I was thinking,' he said, staring straight at me. It was a balmy night, the first warm night of the spring. In the dim light I could see the sweat beads trembling on his upper lip like dewdrops.

'May thinks she can save me,' I said.

'What do you think?' said Stanley after a pause.

I stared at him. I didn't know why he was asking; it could have been for my sake, or it could have been for his. Either way he suddenly looked so tired and heavy-lidded it made me think of the times in the hospital when I'd watched him fall asleep in mid-sentence.

'I'll try anything,' I said.

And then it was Stanley who reached through the bars and took hold of my arm. He was suddenly awake again and he was giving me the same steady gaze he'd given me the first time I'd laid eyes on him.

'Take me with you,' he said, his voice so low it was almost a whisper.

I felt the heat rise up through my cheeks and the back of my neck as far as my scalp. I wasn't sure if he was serious or not, so I just laughed.

'I'm not joking,' he said. 'Why do you think I'm joking?'

'Because it's ridiculous,' I said.

'Bryant's taking Sophie to Sydney,' said Stanley. 'They're getting married.'

'Who's Sophie?'

'Talks Dutch. Tits like footballs.'

'Who says?' I said, still laughing.

'Everybody knows.'

'First I've heard of it,' I said.

'They're just waiting for permission,' said Stanley. 'But he's promised her.'

'Yeah well, Bryant's promised a lot of things to a lot of people,' I said. 'It doesn't mean he's going to keep his word.'

'You could adopt me,' said Stanley. 'Bryant's going to adopt Sophie's sister.'

'Shut up about Bryant,' I said. 'Bryant's a cheat and a liar.'

'He knows about you,' said Stanley. He let go of my arm and fell back on his cot as if he didn't have the strength to sit up any more.

I asked him what he meant.

'Everyone knows,' he said. 'You didn't fuck Hanako at the dance because you don't like doing it with women.'

I didn't bother to deny it because there wasn't any point, particularly not to Stanley. Stanley was the whole cause of my trouble. Ever since he'd shown up at Tatura I'd had the sense that I was a marked man, like I was walking around with a sign on me for everyone to read. It was how Bryant knew and had always known, and that was the reason he'd taken such an interest in me.

'I have to go,' I said.

Stanley didn't say anything. He had his face turned to the wall.

'I can't just take you to Melbourne in my kitbag,' I said.

'You could,' he said, 'if you really wanted to.' He refused to turn around.

I took out a second pack of smokes I had on me and reached down to put it on the floor where Stanley would see it. Then I left.

When I was back on duty patrolling the fence, I passed the spot where Stanley had dug his way underneath the wire. River stones had been brought in, mixed with concrete and dumped in the hole. The sight of them made me stop and stare. It was as if they were a symbol of something I couldn't name, because there were no words for it. As I pictured Stanley scraping the soil away with a frying pan I was suddenly overcome with a sense of futility that went way beyond the dislike I felt for the army in general. This was something more visceral, like heartbreak, or the beginning of the end of my youth.

15

May met me at Spencer Street Station when my train pulled in. As soon as she saw me she came running towards me and almost knocked me down. She wrapped her arms right around me and started swaying as if she wanted to dance.

'There you are,' she said. 'Thank God you've come. I've been battling here on my own for so long.'

When she let me go I took a step back and she looked up at me with a pained expression as if she didn't know whether to slap me or kiss me.

'I'm sorry,' I said. 'It wasn't easy getting leave.'

'You look terrible,' she said.

'I haven't slept since yesterday. I got a lift to Bendigo then I had to wait for a train at four in the morning. You look lovely.' She did. Her skin was glowing as if it was its own source of light.

'Apart from the fact that I bring up my breakfast every morning, I'm fine,' she said, taking hold of my arm.

She steered me out of the station and into a taxi queue.

'I need to brief you,' she said. 'Before you meet my father. There are certain topics of conversation you need to steer clear of.'

'You make it sound like I'm applying for a job.'

'You are.'

We shuffled ahead in the queue. May gripped my arm as if she was afraid I might run away.

'Don't mention Owen,' she said.

I glanced down at her and saw she was about to cry.

'I won't,' I said, holding her close.

'There's still no news of him,' she said.

In the taxi she held my hand and leaned against me, as if we were already married. The taxi driver kept glancing at us in his rear-view mirror and smiling. I wanted to ask him to keep his eyes on the road.

Twenty minutes later we turned into a long, leafy avenue in Kew, then pulled up in front of a big modern pile the colour of marzipan. May's house was not what I expected, but at least it explained the monogrammed notepaper. I was in half a mind to tell the driver to turn around and take me back to the station, but May had me by the coat sleeve and was pulling me out onto the street.

'Come on,' she said. 'You're safe with me.'

'That's what they all say,' said the taxi driver, winking at me as he wrestled the gearstick back into first.

I paused on the driveway to admire the canary-yellow Pontiac parked in the shade at the front of the house.

'Is this our wedding present?' I said.

'Could be,' said May. 'If you play your cards right.'

Before we went inside she diverted me around to the side of the house where she pinned me to a garden wall and pulled my head down to her level so she could kiss me and slide her tongue in between my teeth.

'I'm so happy,' she said once she was finished.

'Me too,' I said, and I was. I'd forgotten how easy it was to be with May. She had such a firm idea of what she wanted, and she didn't make me confused the way Stanley made me confused, because for her wanting something and having it were the same thing.

'Don't let them bludgeon you into seeing things their way,' she said.

'You make them sound like the Gestapo.'

'They *are* the Gestapo. They don't want me to marry you. They think I'm throwing my life away.'

'That makes two of us.'

'What's that supposed to mean?' she said, sounding hurt. She pinched me on my arm through my coat. 'We decided.'

'That was on the telephone.'

'And you said yes,' said May, pinching me some more.

I put my arms up in the air in a gesture of surrender. 'Just joking,' I said.

'Don't make jokes like that in front of my parents,' she said. 'You've got to show them you're man enough to take care of me.'

I wanted to laugh out loud when she put it like that, because I was feeling less manly by the minute and more like a spectator at my own execution.

'What have you told them about me?' I said.

'I've told them to give you a chance,' she said ominously.

I stayed for lunch, a leg of lamb with all the trimmings that Mrs Forbes and May had apparently taken great trouble to prepare. We sat outside on a wide covered verandah and admired the sunlit lawn. For something to say I asked Mr Forbes whether he'd built the house himself.

'No,' he said, without looking up at me. He was a big, bovine man with sandy hair and solid limbs. He seemed shy, like a visitor in his own home. If he turned in my direction he would flutter his eyelids nervously, to avoid seeing me. Mrs Forbes, on the other hand, couldn't take her eyes off me. She kept staring at me with a half-smile on her lips as if she thought everything I had to say was vaguely funny. She was the one May took after. They had the same plumpness and the same pale, freckled skin.

'He builds office buildings,' said May. 'And hotels.'

'I see,' I said, although I had no idea what building office buildings and hotels might involve apart from the exchange of large amounts of money.

'What does your father do?' said May's mother.

'His mother and father abandoned him,' said May, before I could answer. 'I told you.'

I stared at the starched tablecloth while Mrs Forbes continued to smile and Mr Forbes coughed into his serviette.

'I'm so sorry,' said Mrs Forbes.

'It was a long time ago,' I said. I was relieved I'd lied to May about my parents. It meant I wouldn't have to introduce them to Mr and Mrs Forbes and watch them make fools of themselves, which they undoubtedly would have done the minute they realised they were outclassed.

'May tells us you're a guard at an enemy alien camp,' said May's father.

'I am.'

'Guarding Japs,' he said, his disapproval apparent.

'Mostly.'

'Looked after pretty well I hear,' he said.

'It's not too bad.' I wasn't sure where his line of questioning was headed until May suddenly interrupted.

'It's not Arthur's personal responsibility how the camps are run,' she said, glaring at me meaningfully, as if she was warning me to be careful.

'You know our son was captured by the Japs?' said Mr Forbes.

'May told me.'

'You've seen the pictures no doubt, of what the prisoners endured?' said Mr Forbes.

I didn't say anything. I had seen the pictures. I was as shocked and sickened as the next man.

'We hope and pray,' said Mrs Forbes.

I glanced at May. Her eyes were full of tears.

'The point is,' said Mr Forbes, 'what were we doing feeding and clothing the Jap prisoners here, while over there the bastards were working our blokes to death?'

'Stop it, Dad,' said May. 'Please.'

'It's all right,' I said. 'I see your point Mr Forbes.'

'Do you?' he said.

He still wouldn't look at me, so I turned to Mrs Forbes. 'I think if you saw the camp where I'm stationed you'd understand. They're mostly women and children.'

'May tells me you teach them tennis,' said Mrs Forbes. She had stopped eating now and was arranging her knife and fork on her empty plate.

'I do,' I said, feeling suddenly seasick, as if May's light-filled house with its cool flagstones and dreamy lawn had come loose from its moorings and started to drift. A part of me wanted to be back with the kids at Tatura whacking battered tennis balls backwards and forwards in the dust, instead of sitting here on my plush seat fiddling with the silverware.

'Are we ready for dessert?' said Mrs Forbes.

'Always ready for dessert,' said Mr Forbes.

I tried to help May and her mother with the clearing away but they told me to stay where I was so Mr Forbes and I could talk. He offered me a smoke and I thanked him. Then he offered to light it for me. We were both watching the match burn down in the ashtray when he started to speak.

'I never wanted May to join the Land Army,' he said.

'Why not?'

'Because it's back-breaking work. I didn't want her to ruin her health.'

'Actually he was scared I'd marry a farmer,' May called out from the kitchen so we would know she was listening.

Mr Forbes smiled for the first time since we'd sat down to

eat. I took that as a sign he was starting to relax with me, that maybe I'd passed a test.

'She's as stubborn as a mule,' he said.

I tried smiling back at him but it was a waste of time because he was staring out into the trees.

'Do you love her?' he said.

'I think so,' I said. 'Yes.' And I believed it as I said it, even if the next moment I was afraid that Mr Forbes might accuse me of lying.

'You don't sound too confident,' he said.

He finally looked straight at me, challenging me to convince him.

I turned away and stared into the kitchen at May as she helped her mother. After a pause I turned back and faced Mr Forbes.

'She's a very special girl,' I said. 'I'm lucky I found her.'

It seemed to satisfy him. He took a drag on his cigarette and held the smoke in for a while before letting it seep out through his teeth.

'What are your plans then, Arthur?' he said. 'After the army.'

I'd been expecting this question but I still didn't have a ready answer. The truth was that I was less able to think about the future with every passing day. In this sense May's plan to get married and start a family had nothing to do with me. I was essentially along for the ride.

'He's looking for a job,' said May. She and her mother had returned with a cake on a platter and some matching plates. 'Aren't you Arthur?' It was a statement rather than a question.

'I will be,' I said. 'As soon as I get my discharge.'

'I think he should go to work for Ian,' said May. She sat down next to Mr Forbes and slipped her arm through his. 'Even if he just starts out as a driver.'

'Ian is in transport,' said Mrs Forbes, smiling at me in her half-amused way.

'I know,' I said. 'May told me.'

'It's certainly worth considering,' said her father. Again he was staring out at the trees and I had the impression that most of the time he didn't actually listen to May or her mother, that every-thing they said was just background noise to his private musings.

'There are worse things than making a lot of money,' he said. 'But I'm sure you know that.'

He made it sound so easy that I giggled. And that started May and her mother grinning as well, as if what Mr Forbes had said was a family joke they never failed to find amusing.

'I'll take your word for it,' I said.

At which Mr Forbes reached out and slapped me on the arm in a chummy way.

'He's all right,' he said, smiling in May's direction but at the same time fluttering his eyelids so he couldn't actually focus on her.

'I told you,' said May, wolfing down her cake.

'You'll make yourself sick,' said her mother.

'I have a craving for cream,' said May, 'anything with cream in it. I'm like the proverbial cat.'

I exchanged a smile with Mrs Forbes across the table as she handed me a large slice of cake and cream.

'May tells me you're a country boy,' she said.

'I was,' I said, reluctant to elaborate. The key to lying, in my experience, was to stick to generalities.

'Was your father a farmer?' she said.

'No,' I said. 'He did various jobs.'

'How did you feel when your parents left you?' she said.

'Mother,' said May, annoyed. 'What kind of a question is that?'

'It's all right,' I said. I stared at the cake in front of me and took a deep breath before continuing. 'I didn't get on with my parents Mrs Forbes. We had very different ideas about life.'

'Such as?' said Mr Forbes. He too was happily spooning cake into his cavernous mouth.

'They had very limited horizons,' I said. 'They tried to stifle my ambitions.'

'Which were?' Mr Forbes fluttered his eyelids at me.

'When I was twelve years old I wanted to be a designer,' I said.

'What kind of a designer?' said May's mother.

'I wasn't sure,' I said. 'I liked to draw.'

'And you don't any more?' she said.

I looked up from my plate and saw that they were all watching me, waiting for me to trip myself up.

'It was something I grew out of,' I said, wondering if that was in fact the truth, or whether I'd given up out of shame.

'Don't you miss them?' said Mrs Forbes.

'Don't be ridiculous,' said May. 'Of course he misses them.'

She had finished her cake and looked at me now with a half-smile just like her mother's.

'Maybe you can stop interrogating him now,' she said, 'and let me take him for a tour around the garden. We have things to discuss.'

'Would you like some tea first?' said Mrs Forbes hopefully.

'No,' I said. 'Thank you. That was a lovely lunch.'

May was already standing. She came around to my side of the table and took hold of my arm, dragging me to my feet. Her mother watched her, looking vaguely wounded.

'I hope you can stay for dinner,' she said.

'We're going out for dinner,' said May. 'I told you. We're going dancing at The Dug-Out.'

Mrs Forbes raised her eyebrows at May in a hapless way.

'Of course you are,' she said, giving in to her daughter's superior talent for action and decisiveness.

Once we were out in the garden May told me how well I'd done.

'My mother sees the Errol Flynn resemblance,' she said. 'And my father, believe it or not, was on his best behaviour.'

'I'm glad,' I said.

'You don't look it,' said May. 'You look miserable.'

'I haven't even met Ian,' I said. 'How do you know he has a job for me?'

'Because I asked him,' she said, mocking my solemn tone.

'What did he say?'

'He said he's always on the lookout for good men.'

'Who says I'm a good man?'

She took hold of my hand and dragged me along a path through waist-high primroses and azaleas to the back boundary of the garden where she stopped and made me kiss her again.

'Are you sure it's what you want?' she said.

'What do you mean?' I said. I was afraid she was going to change her mind and abandon me.

'I don't want you to wake up one day and regret everything. By then it'll be too late.'

I kissed her again as hard as I could. 'That is never going to happen,' I said. 'Without you I'm completely lost.'

'Thank you,' she said. 'I knew I could trust you.'

'I'll do everything I can to make us happy,' I said, putting my arms around her and holding her so tight that she complained she couldn't breathe.

'You're going to squash the baby,' she said.

I let go of her. She held onto my hand, placing it on her belly.

'It swims like a fish,' she said.

I kept my hand where it was and waited. Talk of the baby made me anxious and excited all at once. I meant what I said when I told her I'd work hard to make us happy, but I also feared that I would fail. I knew nothing about children, only what I'd learned from being a child myself.

'I hope it's a girl,' I said.

'I don't care what it is,' said May. 'I love it already.'

She lifted my hand to her breast and rested it there. And then she kissed me again.

'Am I the first woman you ever kissed?' she said.

I blushed and smiled helplessly at her.

'I thought so,' she said.

The Dug-Out was a servicemen's club in Swanston Street. May wore a dress she'd made herself from shiny navy brocade. Apparently she'd already grown out of all her old dresses. I'd never seen her look so pretty. She had started putting her hair up in a new way that showed off her white neck. Actually it was painful how pretty she looked because I couldn't help noticing the way other men kept staring at her with undisguised interest. It made me realise she was wasted on me. I didn't look at women that way. I didn't look at anyone that way. If a man caught my eye, say on the dance floor, or at the bar where we were lining up for a beer, I was careful not to stare. But that didn't mean I didn't see them. They were everywhere. The streets were full of men, all back from the war, suddenly let loose on the town to make up for all the time they'd lost. I went to bed each night with a head full of drink and catalogued the men I'd seen, comparing them all, unfavourably, to Stanley.

On the second night May came to find me in the guest room and climbed into bed beside me. She was wearing only a sheer dressing-gown with nothing underneath it. I knew that because she took hold of my hand and pressed it between her legs. At the same time she reached down with her other hand and took hold of my cock.

'Will it hurt the baby?' I said, not quite knowing what she intended to do next.

'Don't talk,' she whispered. 'My parents are down the hall.' I went quiet after that, and let her do whatever she wanted. I remember we'd both had a fair bit to drink and that may have helped us to enjoy ourselves. We ended up staying together for the whole night and waking up at dawn in each other's arms. Before she left to go back to her own room May asked me what I'd been dreaming about.

I told her I couldn't remember, which was true.

'You were talking in your sleep,' she said. 'Something about the moon.'

And then it came back to me, how in my dream Stanley and I had been running through the bush, using the light of the moon to see by, when my father had suddenly appeared wearing his policeman's uniform and carrying an enormous sack.

'Actually,' I told May. 'It was about you. How you came into my bed with no clothes on and did things to me no lady should ever do.' I tried to sound more carefree than I felt.

'You'd know of course,' she said. 'From your vast experience of ladies.'

'They're queuing up,' I said, mimicking the way Stanley talked. 'Every day of the goddamned week.' I even borrowed his accent because I liked the sound of it so much.

May laughed and called me a liar, then she left me alone to sleep some more before breakfast. Except that I was already wide-awake, and in a high state of apprehension. It was as if I could see my whole future stretched out before me, nights in bed with May, days on the road in her brother's trucks, birthdays and Christmases with May's mother and father in their beautiful wedding-cake house. It was hard to know if it was a vision of paradise or something much more sinister. Either way it made me want to pack my bags immediately and flee.

Of course I stayed, because there was breakfast to eat and small talk to be exchanged with Mrs Forbes, and then there was Mr Forbes's standing offer to drive me to the railway station on his way to work so I could catch my train back to camp.

May and I sat in the back seat of the Pontiac, while Mr and Mrs Forbes sat in the front. I don't remember very much of what was said, only that I agreed to leave the wedding arrangements entirely to May and her mother.

'Are you religious?' said Mrs Forbes.

'No.'

'We're Anglican,' she said.

I could see Mr Forbes staring at me in the rear-view mirror while we were pulled up at some traffic lights. It was easy to tell that he didn't really like me.

'I can change,' I said.

May laughed and squeezed my hand and I squeezed hers back half-heartedly while the car took off again, its beautiful motor humming like a bass note.

'You like that sound?' said Mr Forbes.

'Very much.'

'I think you two are going to get along just fine,' said Mrs Forbes, reaching across to give her husband's knee a squeeze. Then she turned and offered me another one of her half-smiles.

16

Stanley was already out of the lock-up by the time I got back to Tatura. I saw him on morning roll call. He was standing with his mother, holding her arm as if she needed restraining. They listened while Hollows made a speech up the front of the assembly. He was standing on his podium and shouting into the stiff breeze.

'Despite the war having ended last month,' he said, 'it will be many long weeks before any of you will be able to leave here, mainly because of the difficult situation that Japan now finds itself in as a defeated and occupied country. Bear in mind that Japan is now facing the coming northern winter without fuel, without basic infrastructure, without food supplies, and, crucially for you, without shipping.' He went on to repeat his daily warning to the internees to remain patient and calm.

After he'd finished speaking and dismissed the parade,

Stanley's mother seemed confused. It was only after Stanley shouted something at her in Japanese that she moved, but she appeared to have forgotten which direction to go in. Stanley allowed her to cling to his shirt-tails as they walked away, as if he was now the parent and she the child.

Riley and I stood watching until the last of the internees had returned to their compounds to wait out another day.

'Why is Stanley out of the lock-up?' I said. 'Perkins told me he had three weeks.'

'His mother got him out,' said Riley. 'She said she'd do herself in if they didn't let him go.'

'Christ,' I said. I remembered the letter Stanley had written to me explaining his secret mission. He'd told me there were things going on in the camp that I would never understand. It was suddenly very clear to me that this was true, that Stanley's real life was hidden from me.

'Why can't they all just go home?' I said, in an exasperated way.

Riley glanced at me, uncertain whether to take me seriously or not. I was not given to expressing sympathy with the Japs, even if I sometimes felt inclined to.

'Bloody good question,' he said.

'Is it true that Bryant's going to marry one of them?' I said. It wasn't something I could ask Bryant to his face.

'That's just more of Bryant's bullshit,' he said. 'He's got two or three different girls convinced that he's going to marry them and take them away from all this. You have to give him full marks for effort.'

'Shouldn't somebody let the girls know?'

Riley laughed. 'You volunteering?'

When I told Bryant I was getting married he laughed. 'Who to?'

'My girl,' I said.

It was late. We were in our hut as usual playing cards and drinking. Donohue was there and so was McMaster.

'I had a bet on you'd made her up,' said Donohue.

I went to my bunk and retrieved a photograph of May and her parents posed in front of the marzipan house. May had given it to me as a souvenir. On the back she'd written *En famille at Chateau Forbes*. Donohue inspected it for a moment then passed it to McMaster who peered at it over his glasses.

'Just like I told you,' said McMaster. 'She'll be the making of you.' He looked up at me and smiled. 'You're doing the right thing.'

'Thanks,' I said. He seemed to have kept the fact of May's pregnancy to himself, and for that I was grateful.

Bryant snatched the photo out of his hand and took a close look at it.

'I'm disappointed,' he said.

'Why's that?' I said.

'You're settling,' he said. 'Before you even know what's available. It's like buying a new car. You have to compare and contrast.'

'I know quality when I see it,' I said. I was feeling brazen because of the rum, and this was the first chance I'd had to even up the score with Bryant on account of all the stories he'd been spreading about Hanako and me. It didn't matter that they were true.

He laughed again, this time throwing his head back and holding his belly with his free hand as if it hurt him to laugh so hard.

'What's so funny?' I said.

Bryant finished laughing and wiped his nose on the sleeve of his shirt. 'Did you fuck her yet?' he said.

'Jesus Bryant,' said McMaster.

'Simple question,' said Bryant.

'Yeah,' I said. 'I did.' Because of a pressure that was building up behind my eyes I couldn't see my cards any more. They were just a blur.

'Good for you,' said Donohue.

'She any good?' said Bryant. He slapped his losing cards down on the table then lit himself a fag.

'None of your business,' I said.

'Fair enough,' he said. He was smiling at me now with his eyes narrowed to keep the smoke out of them. 'But on a scale of ten, what would you give her?'

'Shut up Bryant,' said Donohue. 'Why can't you just leave the kid alone?'

'Because I don't like to see him miss out on all the other fuckable women there are out there,' said Bryant. 'It's a bloody tragedy.'

'Nine,' I said.

'Liar,' said Bryant. He stared hard at the family photograph again then handed it back to me. At the same time McMaster showed his hand with nothing in it. He'd been bluffing, which he was very good at. Nobody was better. Bryant flipped his hand over, a pair of threes.

'The best fuck I ever had was Lizzie Randall,' said Donohue. 'She was twenty-nine years old and I was eighteen.'

'There's a lot to be said for older women,' said Bryant.

McMaster was gathering up the cards. He stared contemptuously at Bryant over the top of them.

'You can't help yourself can you,' said McMaster.

'Not if it's on offer,' said Bryant.

'That includes taking advantage of a woman who is mentally unstable?' said McMaster.

'She made up for it in other ways,' said Bryant, taking a long drink of rum then sloshing some more into everyone else's glasses. As he put the bottle down he looked straight at me and grinned. 'It's all those acrobatic tricks she learned in the circus.'

Donohue leaned across to me grinning. 'You missed a bit of drama the other night,' he told me. 'Stanley's mother showed up on the doorstep here with hardly any clothes on. Asking for Bryant.'

'Riley told me,' I said, even though he hadn't. My stomach churned as if I was about to be sick.

'Bet you he didn't tell you what happened next,' said Donohue.

'I don't want to know,' I said. I was having trouble staying in my seat. The night was chilly but I'd broken out in a sweat inside my uniform.

'She was an eight,' said Bryant, running his tongue along his top teeth and sucking his breath in at the same time.

I don't really know what happened next. I must have jumped

up and thrown my whole weight at Bryant because he fell back in his chair and knocked his head on the floor and suddenly there was blood all over his shirt and he was screaming at me, calling me a fucking faggot cunt and swinging at me with his fists. He landed a few cracking punches before McMaster and Donohue managed to pull him off me and after that I passed out. I woke up half an hour later in the infirmary with a fractured collarbone and a broken nose and a right eye that refused to open. It was a miracle, Matron Conlon told me, that I hadn't lost it altogether.

Bryant was apparently even worse off. He hadn't fully recovered after banging his head—he kept vomiting and lapsing in and out of consciousness—so they'd trucked him all the way to Bendigo to have him looked after there. I was glad, although I didn't tell that to Matron Conlon because I knew she didn't approve of violence.

'He had it coming,' was all I said, before she told me to stop talking and get some rest.

For the next couple of days I lay in bed and waited for Stanley to come and see me. When he failed to show up I fell into a state of such dejection that even Matron Conlon could no longer stand it.

'I suppose you're missing your sweetheart,' she said to me on the third evening. She was changing the dressing on my damaged eye. 'Would you like me to telephone and tell her you're on the road to recovery?'

'No,' I said. 'She'll only worry.'

'I hear you're getting married,' she said.

I nodded.

'You're too young if you ask me,' she said.

A lump rose in my throat and my chin started to tremble. Matron Conlon cupped my face in her hands.

'I think you need to tell me what's going on,' she said, staring hard at me out of her rheumy eyes. 'What on earth convinced you to take on the likes of Bryant? The man's built like an ox.'

'I wasn't thinking,' I said.

She let go of my face and finished bandaging my eye, then patted the top of my head as if I was a much younger boy.

'There are easier ways to get out of the army,' she said. 'You're lucky you're not up on a criminal charge.'

'Can you get a message to Stanley?' I said, blurting it out. It had occurred to me that I may not have a chance to see him again if things turned out badly with Bryant.

'Sure I can try,' she said.

Stanley appeared in my doorway the following day. I was climbing back into bed after a trip to the toilet—taking it in stages, like an old man.

'You want a hand?' he said.

He was dressed up, in a tie and a lightweight grey suit that was one size too big for him. He wore a pair of filthy sandshoes. My first instinct was to cross the room and put my arms around him, but there was another patient in the six-bed ward, an asthmatic named Ryan, and I was afraid he might see us.

'No thanks,' I said. I settled myself under the covers and motioned for Stanley to come closer. 'Shut the door,' I said.

He kicked the door closed and came over to stand beside me.

'What happened to you?' he said.

'I cut myself shaving,' I said. I didn't want to tell him about my fight with Bryant, or what had provoked it.

He took out a pack of cigarettes and offered me one.

'Thanks,' I said. He lit both cigarettes at once and handed one to me. All the time I was trying to control the urge to take hold of his hand.

'I guess this is goodbye,' he said, flashing me a ravishing smile.

'I'm not dying,' I said. 'Just wounded in action.'

'I can't stay long,' he said, turning his head away. I admired his smooth jaw and the line of his chin.

'Why not?' I said.

I didn't want him to leave. I wanted him to climb into my bed so I could lie with him the same way I had before. I wanted him to kiss me again on the cheek.

'Compound meeting,' he said.

'What about?'

'The latrines. It's always about the latrines.'

He took a couple of long drags on his cigarette before he spoke again.

'How was Melbourne?'

'Fine.'

'I was wondering if you've read anything, or heard anything,' he said.

'What about?'

'Closing the camp,' he said.

'Nothing,' I said. 'But if I do I'll let you know.'

He turned to face me. His smile had vanished. He put his hand over the top of mine and stared at me with such heart-stopping earnestness I thought I would faint.

'I'll always remember you,' he said. 'I want you to know that.'

He leaned over and brushed his lips against mine. 'Sayonara,' he said.

I tried to stop him from walking away. I struggled out of bed and followed him to the door, grabbing hold of his jacket and tugging to slow him down, but he was too quick for me and he shrugged me off. Just as he opened the door into the reading room Matron Conlon appeared on her way out of her office. She looked at Stanley, then at me standing behind him, tears brimming in my one good eye.

'I told you to cheer him up,' she said.

Stanley didn't say a word. He marched out past her office and turned the corner into the laundry. I heard the tin door slam behind him.

'Get some slippers on,' said Matron Conlon.

I stared down at my bare feet.

'I don't want you catching pneumonia on top of everything else.' She stepped forward, put her arm around my waist, and guided me back to my bed.

'Are you two still friends?' she said, tucking me in.

I couldn't bring myself to answer her.

Eventually, when my eye became infected, I was sent away from Tatura to a veterans' hospital in Heidelberg, where May visited me every other day and lectured the doctors on how to save my sight.

My army career ended as ignobly as it had begun, with me laid up in yet another hospital bed contemplating this latest demonstration of my poor character. When my dishonourable discharge came through at the end of October I showed the papers to May and told her I would understand if she wanted to change her mind about us getting married. But May just folded the papers and told me she didn't give a damn what the army said about me.

'I'm glad you're out of that place,' she said. 'Now you can forget about the war and start to live your life.' She proceeded to tell me how the wedding plans were shaping up and how I would need to get fitted for a suit as soon as I was out of hospital.

'I've already got you a shirt,' she said. 'I bought it the same time as I bought Ian's.'

'I'm sorry for being so useless,' I said. 'I haven't even bought you a ring.'

'We can choose one together,' she said.

As soon as my army pay came through I gave it to her to cover the cost, except that even then I had to borrow an extra hundred pounds from May's father to get her the ring she wanted.

'I'm very grateful,' I told Mr Forbes at the wedding. 'I owe you a great deal.'

'Don't you forget it,' he said.

His eyelids fluttered as he gazed across the heads of all the wedding guests. Ian stood beside him in a shirt that matched mine but was considerably bigger. A loud, brash man, he was as gregarious as his father was reticent.

I asked Ian if there was any advice he could give me. 'You've known May a lot longer than I have,' I said.

He chuckled and took a sip of his beer. 'She's an open book,' he said. 'What you see is what you get. And then some.' He made a gesture over his own considerable paunch to make fun of May's ballooning belly.

May appeared from behind me and linked her arm through mine. She'd changed out of her voluminous wedding dress into something low-cut and blousy that showed off her milky bosoms. 'What lies are you telling him about me?' she asked her brother.

'I'm just telling him what a child you are,' said Ian.

May beamed up at me and clung even tighter to my arm. 'That's why I need a big strong man to look after me,' she said.

'Where?' I said, glancing around me as if I was looking for someone. 'Is he in the room?'

Of course I meant it as a joke and everyone laughed. But at the same time I was only putting into words what I really felt. I'd married May for a number of reasons, but none of them had anything to do with feelings of power or adequacy.

'Bad boy,' said May, pinching me on the cheek. 'I might just call the whole thing off.'

'Too late now,' I said.

I wrote to Stanley at the beginning of December to tell him how sorry I was that I hadn't been able to see him again before leaving the camp.

They turfed me out of the army while I was still in the hospital. McMaster sent me my things, so I have your stories. Please let me know if you'd like me to return them to you at any time, or if there is anything else you would like me to get for you. I will try my best to help you in any way I can. I'm living with my wife's family at the moment but from next month May and I will be moving to a new place. Please write, Arthur.

And then I printed out the address of the house that Mr Forbes had bought for May and me to live in. It was two streets away from Ian's truck depot in Hawthorn.

Before I posted the letter I included a photograph I'd taken of Stanley and some of the kids all gathered around the net on the tennis court at Tatura. I wrote *Always in my thoughts* on the back and slipped it into the envelope before taking the letter down to the post box at the end of the street on my way to work. Ian had hired me to drive deliveries around the city, mostly furniture for offices and shops, occasionally heavy machinery for factories that were either closing down after the war or switching to civilian manufacturing.

I think that first Christmas with May and her family marked the beginning of my posthumous life, the one in which I was a new man, unrecognisable even to myself. There was nothing exceptional about this feeling of estrangement, this sense of suspended reality. Every man expecting his first child must feel that his life is about to become unfamiliar and difficult to chart. But added to that there was the sense that the aftermath of the war was likely to be cruel and prolonged. Owen had not come home and the exact manner of his death was still unknown. May continued to cry whenever his name was mentioned. At the same time as I grieved for her I also mourned for my own losses. I waited for news of Stanley like a dog waits to hear the sound of his master's voice.

That was what I was doing on the occasions when May caught me out and asked me where I'd gone. *I wish I could bring you back* was how she put it, as if I was a man who's heart has stopped beating.

'I married you,' I told her. 'What more do you want?'

To which she always replied the same way. *You,* she said. *I want you.*

Of course I knew what she was getting at, never more so than on the day she gave birth to our son. I visited her in the hospital and she showed me the sleeping baby. My first thought was to bolt. I had a vision of myself fleeing the building and running all the way back to Tatura to tell Stanley it was a boy.

17

Stanley finally replied to my letter on May 16th, 1946, almost a year to the day since the first time I'd met him. I have kept this letter, along with the photographs of him I mentioned before, because it reminds me of how my life turned so suddenly to ruin on the day I received it.

> *Dear Arthur,*
>
> *I don't know if this letter will ever reach you but I must write to ask for you to help me. As you can see I am still in camp with my family but I am trying to get out so I can travel to Melbourne and meet you. My plan is to work for the Americans in Australia and after to go back to America where I know very well. Also I have a cousin in Chicago who is attending a college, which is my dream as I told you. Unfortunately I can*

convince nobody here at all. The authorities says I must stay
with my family and depart back to Japan with them. But this
is not my wish. I have no life in Japan and no money and no
job and Japan is a ruined country as you know. I beg you to
talk to Colonel Hollows and tell him you know my real char-
acter and that I am not a dangerous person.
Your true and faithful friend,
Stanley Ueno.

The letter was weeks late arriving. I didn't finally receive it
until late September after it had coursed through all the official
channels before washing up on my doorstep like a bit of debris
from a shipwreck. By then I was well advanced on the project of
rehabilitating myself. Marriage was to have been the start of my
new life—my chance, as the Forbes family put it, to settle down
and build something solid and respectable. I knew they were
right, just as I knew I could throw it all away at any moment,
given a good enough excuse. In this sense Stanley's letter was
exactly what I'd been waiting for. I read it through three or four
times while May was in the backyard hanging out the washing.
I could see her through the kitchen window pegging my work
shirts together in her methodical way, with their arms dangling
down like dead men. By the time she'd lifted the empty wash
basket onto her hip I was resolved to go.

I spent that day searching high and low for enough fuel to get
me to Tatura, then I made my getaway the following morning,
while May and Stuart were still asleep. Before I left I wrote my
wife a note saying there was something I had to do. *I'll explain*

everything when I get back, I lied. I scribbled her name on the front then stuck the note under the sugar bowl on the kitchen table. The truck was parked out in the backyard. I threw my bag in the passenger side and climbed into the driver's seat. Before I turned the ignition I sat for a while staring at the sleeping house and wondered, yet again, why I was like this. Other men stayed where they were and endured—that was the difference between them and me. For a whole year I'd tried to settle down and turn myself into a blameless family man, and by and large I'd succeeded. Except that my wife wasn't a complete fool. For all the time we'd been married, and even before that, May had sensed I was faking.

'Are you sorry we met?' she said. It was one of those weekends soon after Stuart's birth when we'd argued for two whole days—about small things: the lawn, the leaking bathroom tap, the baby's refusal to sleep.

'I don't know what you mean,' I said.

'Sometimes it's like you're not even here,' she said. She had Stuart in her arms. He was whining and flailing his arms and legs like a helpless beetle. 'I mean you sit there in your chair but you're miles away.'

'I'm sorry,' I said.

She stood up and started to rock the baby violently.

'I wish I knew how to reach you,' she said.

I hid behind my newspaper. 'I don't have to listen to this,' I said.

May tried her hardest to make me. Persistence was the principle she lived by. She'd married me against the advice of her parents just to prove a point. She was going to keep us together come hell or high water, because that would show how strong she was, and because she loved me, which was the really agonising part.

'I loved you from the first moment I saw you,' she told me. She said it so often it became a kind of joke between us.

I knew what that was like, because it had happened to me. It was like being upended all of a sudden, having your internal organs forcefully rearranged. I had only to remember the exact moment Stanley had taken his hat off in the hallway of the infirmary for my blood to halt in my veins.

'Do you love me?' she said.

I told her to stop asking me that. I said there were countries where the word for love was hardly spoken but that didn't mean it wasn't there. It was something I'd made up to impress her with my sophistication about these things. Why she didn't slap me in the face I can't imagine.

'Do you love Stuart?'

'That's a ridiculous question,' I said. 'There isn't a word that describes what I feel for Stuart.'

'You never touch him,' she said.

It was true. I wasn't a demonstrative father. I preferred to watch the baby rather than to hold him, and sometimes, if he was in any pain or discomfort, I couldn't even bear to watch him. But this was not from a lack of love. It was from a fear that I might damage him.

Years later Stuart would always swear that he could remember the day I left him. He said he'd woken in his cot and watched through the window as I drove away. But I never believed him.

I told him his mother must have filled him in on the gruesome details way after the event, because he'd only been a baby at the time.

'I refused to sleep in my cot after that,' he said. 'I would only sleep in her bed.'

'That's your story,' I laughed, meaning to make things easier between us. Except that my attempts at humour never worked. He didn't find anything amusing about my desertion. For him it would always be a betrayal, whereas for me it went beyond that. That I was so eager to sacrifice my family for Stanley's sake went to the very heart of my madness back then.

I wanted to tell Stuart not to take anything I'd done in the past personally. I wanted to tell him, without going into the particulars, that the war was to blame for my shameful behaviour, but I didn't think he'd believe me for one moment, let alone find it in his heart to forgive me.

I started up the truck engine and listened to it turning over. The throaty rumble of Ian's one-and-a-half-ton Ford was the sweetest sound I knew at that time. It was the sound of what passed for my soul, which had always started singing the minute I was in motion, propelled along by the raw power of pistons and gasoline.

I never thought of turning back. I wasn't even sad. As soon as I was out on the main road I pushed the accelerator flat to the floor and fled the scene, a thief, an absconder. It wasn't for the first time. I'd left my parents in a similar state of high dudgeon, packed my bags and walked out of the house without a word. In a sense I'd run away from the Air Force too, and then from the army. I'd come to the conclusion that it was probably the thing I did best. I think I even yelled out loud through the open driver's-side window because of my joy at being on the loose again, and because Stanley was waiting to meet me at the other end of the road.

I imagined walking into Tatura and walking out again with Stanley at my side. I dreamed of sailing away to America with him on the first leaky boat we could find. It was the kind of fantasy I'd spun in my head before, whenever Stanley had talked about his American travels. It was a sign of my limitless capacity for self-delusion that I never bothered to check on Stanley's whereabouts before I set out to rescue him that day. But then I'd never let the facts get in the way of my grand purpose before. Facts were for lesser men, office clerks and bank managers, and I must have convinced myself somehow that I was immune to them.

18

It is true that it was easy to abandon my wife and child, that I felt no remorse. All I can say in my defence is that I was in the grip of a type of delirium at the time, the nature of which remains obscure to me even now. Back then I had only one idea in my head, which was to reach Stanley before he was sent away. If I felt any guilt it was only on his behalf, because I'd neglected him, made a sacrifice of him for the sake of my new respectability. It helped that marriage and fatherhood no longer felt like a blessing to me. By the time I received Stanley's letter from Tatura I had started to believe it was a curse. That was why I didn't wake May up to tell her to her face where I was going, and why I never looked back once I was gone.

An hour after I set off from Hawthorn it started to rain, a hard, freezing, unseasonable downpour that went on and on. I drove fast with the rain slamming on the roof so loud it drowned out any other sound. I wasn't really thinking what I would do once I reached Tatura. All I was worried about was how fast I could get there. I stopped only once to get something to eat because I was afraid of falling asleep at the wheel. I'd barely slept the night before. May had been up with Stuart three times and then she'd brought him into bed with us where he'd fussed and squirmed.

It was only when I finally arrived at Tatura at around six o'clock in the morning that I realised the mistake I'd made. The place had been emptied out the way a house is vacated when the owners sell up. I pulled up at the gate expecting to be met and asked my business, but found it unmanned. Even after I sounded my horn nobody came to meet me. Eventually I had to get out of the truck and slosh through the mud to open the outer gate myself, and then make my way to the guardhouse where I shouted out from the bottom of the steps to anyone who might hear me. A guard finally appeared at the door, annoyed that I'd called him out into the rain. It was Davies. He peered out at me through his steamy glasses.

'You're back,' he said.

'Where is everyone?' I said.

'Gone.'

I walked over to the inner fence. Through the pelting rain I could just make out the deserted parade ground and the huts in the distance, all closed up. Davies followed me and held an umbrella over the both of us.

'When?' I said.

'The last lot left three days ago.'

'Where did they go?'

'Sydney,' he said. 'Come in out of the wet.'

Once we were inside the guardhouse he handed me a mug of hot, black, sugary tea from a thermos on his desk, then he offered me a smoke.

'Is Colonel Hollows here?' I said.

'Gone with the first group.'

'What are you blokes doing?'

'Guarding army property,' he said without smiling. Behind his glasses I couldn't tell if he meant this to be humorous or not.

'Who from?' I said.

Davies didn't answer. He just took a drag on his smoke and stared out the grimy window at the rain.

'There's a couple still in the infirmary,' he said. 'Matron refused to let them go on the transports.'

'Who are they?' I said.

'There's an old fella with pneumonia,' said Davies, 'and a woman.'

'What's her name?' I said, half-hoping it was Stanley's mother.

'A Dutch East Indies girl,' said Davies. 'Ten months pregnant.'

'Sophie?'

'That's the one.'

'I'd like to see them,' I said.

'What for?'

I didn't know how to answer him so I just sat there smoking and drinking my tea.

'You look completely done in,' he said.

'I had an early start,' I said. 'I'm on a run up to Albury with some farm machinery.'

For a moment I thought of telling him about Stanley's letter. He'd been kind to me in the past. But when I saw the way he was staring at me through his greasy glasses I changed my mind.

'You didn't see the papers?' he said.

'I've stopped reading them,' I said.

He glanced at his watch. 'Have a rest now,' he said. 'Then I'll take you over to get some breakfast when my relief gets here.'

I went and lay down on his bunk and was asleep almost immediately. When I finally woke up it was lunchtime and a stranger was on duty, a thin stick of a man who introduced himself as Lovell.

'We decided to leave you be,' he said.

'Thanks,' I said. 'Davies said I might be able to eat something at the mess.'

'You can always ask.'

I saw through the window that it had finally stopped raining. I remembered how the parade ground had always turned instantly from a dustbowl into a bog in heavy rain and how the kids had liked to play in the mud, digging trenches that filled with filthy water and making mock battlegrounds.

'Did you see them go?' I said.

'I did. Good riddance if you ask me.'

From the top of the guardhouse I spied the familiar kitchen chimney. Once I was through the inner gate I marched towards it, as if I was back in uniform and reporting for duty, but the silence stopped me in my tracks. I stopped and listened to the wind wheeling across the empty space carrying nothing but its own noise—no human speech, no footsteps, no laughter.

The mess hall was empty too, except for a man and a woman I didn't know. They were sitting together at one of only three remaining tables. All of the other tables had been removed. They looked up as I approached.

'Who are you?' said the woman.

'Arthur Wheeler.'

A patch on her sleeve said she was a warden.

'I was a guard here. I came back to see everyone,' I said, aware of how stupid I sounded now that it had turned out there was nobody here.

'Too late,' said the warden, stating the obvious. Her voice was as deep as a man's.

'Shame,' I said. 'I was just passing through.'

The man, a cook, offered me a seat and then went into the kitchen to get me something to eat. The warden went back to mopping up her gravy with a thick slice of bread. Her fingers were stumpy, with square ends and raw nails.

'When did you leave here?' she said.

'A year ago.'

'Well before my time.'

She finished eating and wiped her hands on her handkerchief. 'My name's Upton,' she said.

'Pleased to meet you,' I said.

The cook returned from the kitchen carrying a plate of bangers and mash and some cutlery. 'No seconds,' he said, placing them in front of me.

He sat down again to finish his own meal.

'Thanks,' I said.

There was a pause while Upton watched me eating. 'What are you doing now you're out of the army?' she said.

'I'm in the transport business,' I said through a mouthful. 'With my brother-in-law.'

'You're not married,' she said. 'You're just a kid.'

'Married with a son,' I said and felt a sudden constriction in my throat that made me gag.

The cook poured me a cup of water and passed it across the table. I took a sip and waited for my throat to clear.

'Why have they sent everyone to Sydney?' I said.

'They're headed back to Nippon,' said Upton. 'Them and a mob of the single men from Hay.'

'When?' I said.

'Around about now,' said the cook.

'How do you know?' I said.

'It's just what we were told,' he said.

I continued to eat but it was like swallowing stones.

'How do you know it's true?' I said.

It was an angry thing to say. I watched the cook and Upton exchange a glance.

'Calm down,' said the cook, smiling at me warily. He stood up and disappeared behind the servery for a moment, returning with a copy of the *Tatura Guardian*.

'It could be just a rumour,' I said. I'd broken out in a sweat by then. I took my handkerchief and wiped my face with it.

The cook found the article he was looking for and handed me

the paper, pointing to the photograph of a group of Japs sitting in the dirt on top of their suitcases. I knew all of them. *Japs on a Slow Boat to Tokyo* said the headline. I read the story twice then returned the paper to him.

'Where are you headed?' said Upton.

'What do you mean?'

'You said you were passing through,' she said. She glanced at the cook again but he had his gaze fixed on me as if he was afraid I was going to jump him.

'Sydney,' I said. If my object was to see Stanley there seemed no option but to keep driving.

I turned to Upton and made an effort to smile. 'I'd like to see Matron Conlon before I leave,' I said.

'I'll take you there,' said Upton. 'When you've finished eating.'

'I've finished,' I said, spooning the last of the mashed potato into my mouth and swallowing so fast I almost choked.

Upton escorted me over to the hospital as if I was a prisoner.

'Make sure you tell someone when you're leaving,' she said.

'I will. Thanks.'

The warden glanced sideways at me.

'Are you going to be all right?' she said without the least trace of kindness.

'Fine.'

'Does your family know where you are?'

I laughed. For a second I thought she was asking whether my parents knew my whereabouts, as if I was sixteen again and fresh out of home.

'I'm not here to cause any trouble,' I said. 'If that's what you think.'

Upton stared at me.

'What sort of trouble could you cause?' she said.

We were approaching the infirmary by then. As soon as Matron Conlon saw me she rushed down the front steps and threw herself at me, smelling sweetly of cough lollies and gin.

'Here's a sight for sore eyes,' she said.

Upton seemed satisfied that I was who I said I was. Even so she lingered while Matron Conlon held me at arm's length and took a good look at me.

'What on earth are you doing back here now?' said Matron Conlon. 'Sure they've all gone.'

'I know. The warden's just told me.'

Matron Conlon turned to Upton. 'It's quite all right to leave him with me. We've a bit to catch up on.'

The warden stayed put.

Matron grabbed me and squeezed me to her ample side. 'What did you want to go off and marry for?' she said. 'It broke my heart in two.'

'I didn't mean to.'

'Isn't that what a man would say,' she said, addressing Upton. 'I didn't mean to.'

Upton said she would be in her hut if I needed anything further and walked off. It was Matron Conlon's cue to march me up the stairs and into her office. In the past she'd always kept everything clean and tidy but now there was a mountain of papers on her desk and a crate of empty gin bottles beside her chair. She shut the door firmly behind us and crossed to the glass medicine cabinet by the window. She took out a couple of tin mugs and a bottle and poured us both a drink.

'That warden's a nasty piece of work,' she said. 'You should've seen the way she treated the little children. It was like she was rounding up a mob of sheep, snapping at their heels, shoving them when they didn't want to move. Course they didn't want to move. They had them sitting out on the parade ground on their suitcases for most of the day, the poor little mites.'

She paused to sip her gin and watched me gulp mine down. On top of the tasteless bangers and mash it made me queasy.

'I had a letter from Stanley,' I said, 'telling me to come.'

'Did you now?'

'I only just got it. Otherwise I would have come earlier.'

The gagging in my throat had come back so it took all of my concentration just to get enough air.

In the meantime Matron Conlon had lit herself a smoke. She handed me the packet and waited while I did the same.

'It wouldn't have made any difference,' she said. She helped herself to some more gin while her tears dripped onto her uniform. When she tried to wipe them off I saw how badly her hand was shaking.

'Davies says you kept some of them,' I said.

She managed the saddest of smiles. She'd aged since I'd last seen her. Her red hair had thinned and her skin had an unhealthy blush around the cheeks and nose, the same as my father's had, and for the same reason.

'Two souls,' she said. 'Out of all those hundreds.'

At that moment there was a knock on the door and Matron motioned me to get up and answer it. Sophie was standing outside in the corridor. I'd never actually met her before but I knew who she was. I'd seen her often enough in the mess and at roll call, and Donohue had never tired of talking about her. She was a round girl with a face as flat as a plate and eyes so black and glossy they looked like jewels. Her breasts and her swollen belly seemed too heavy for her short legs to support.

'Christ,' I said. 'What happened to you?'

Sophie stood with her feet planted firmly apart and her hands on her hips. She looked straight past me at Matron Conlon with an expression bordering on panic.

'Sorry,' she said in a whisper. 'I thought it was him.'

'You remember Arthur?' said Matron Conlon.

Sophie glanced at me and smiled in a disappointed way, then turned herself around and swayed away down the verandah with her fat arms swinging.

I sat down again opposite Matron Conlon.

'Who's the father?' I said.

'I'll give you one guess,' said Matron Conlon. She expelled a cloud of smoke that rose and made a halo around her head.

'I thought they were getting married,' I said.

'So did she.'

'Where is he?'

'God only knows. It's a shame really that you didn't do him a permanent injury.' She finished her cigarette and stubbed it out viciously.

'She only agreed to stay behind if I promised to track him

down,' she said. 'But sure was I going to send her off to die by the roadside somewhere between here and Sydney?'

'Did you find him?'

'Not so far.'

'Who's the other one?'

'Mr Nakadai,' she said. 'I wouldn't let them take a man in his condition. It's the same thing as murder. I told them they might as well just put a bullet in him because he'd be dead anyway before they could get him on their bally boat.'

'What about Stanley's mother?'

'She went quietly,' said Matron Conlon. 'It was Stanley who made the most noise. He locked himself in his hut. His mother was the one who persuaded him to give himself up.'

I didn't say anything for a long time. All I could do was finish my cigarette and stub it out in the overflowing ashtray. 'Now what do I do?' I said finally.

She stared at me out of her kindly brown eyes and smiled. 'You'd do better to forget about him.'

'I can't.'

She reached out and touched my cheek and my heart filled like a balloon about to burst.

'Try,' she said.

I stood up and handed my mug back to her.

Matron Conlon didn't follow me out. The last I saw of her she was standing at the window of her office staring out at me. She raised a hand to her lips and kissed her fingertips and then she placed her palm flat against the dirty glass.

I went around the side of the infirmary and stood there for a minute or so crying uncontrollably, partly for Stanley, but mostly out of panic. I had no choice now but to keep travelling. I couldn't turn back down the road to May and Stuart. I couldn't tell May the truth about where I'd been and why, because I knew what she'd say. She'd say that problems like mine couldn't be fixed overnight. And then she'd say she loved me, because that was what she always said, making it sound like an addiction. I'd heard my mother say the same thing to my father more than once, *I love you*, as if nothing he could do would ever make her stop.

19

I drove for two days, pulling over to the side of the road to sleep, stopping in towns along the way to eat. In my delirium I took no notice of the names of any of them or what I ate or who I spoke to. All I saw was the way the country rolled by hour after hour in light that kept changing the shapes and shadows of everything. I wasn't journeying in real time so much as spiralling in inner space, returning again and again to the same moments from my past: Stanley standing naked while Matron Conlon washed him, for example, or the sight of him in his infirmary bed with the sun streaming through the window. The images seemed to mean something different each time they recurred. By the time I reached Sydney I could no longer remember what day it was, or how long I'd been away from home, although it already seemed like years.

At a petrol station in Rushcutters Bay I stopped to wash and shave and change into some clean work overalls I kept in the truck. In the cracked mirror of the station restroom I saw not the madman I undoubtedly was by then, but a well-meaning youth with an honest gaze and a winning smile. After I was done admiring my disguise I drove straight to the docks down at Circular Quay and inquired about a Jap ship. I couldn't pronounce the name, I told them, but the cargo was unmistakable. When the shipping clerk refused to reveal what he knew, I explained that I was a driver for a Melbourne transport company with a couple of stray Jap enemy aliens in my load who'd been left behind at the camp for health reasons but were now fit to travel.

'But if I'm too late, mate, I'll just have to hand them over to you blokes so you can find them another boat.'

He went off to check with his superior. I could see them talking through a glass partition in the centre of the office. I lit a smoke and waved when they glanced in my direction, my heart bouncing around in my ribcage like an India rubber ball.

Eventually the shipping clerk came back with the name of the ship written on a slip of paper. He handed it to me as if it was something unspeakable.

'You're lucky,' he said.

'Why's that?'

'Sails in the morning. Out of Woolloomooloo.'

It was already late afternoon. I drove around from the Quay to the docks on the other side of the Domain and found a place to leave the truck. I saw straightaway where the *Daikai Maru* was tied up because there was a small crowd gathered two or three deep along a mesh wire fence at the end of the naval dockyards. The boat listed at the very end of the wharf, battered and barely seaworthy, with a rickety gangplank dangling off its side. I counted six machine-gunners stationed along the jetty beside it. You could hear the crowd half a mile away calling out like it was a football match. About twenty cops were lined just the other side of the fence, keeping an eye on things.

I calculated that if I could somehow talk my way inside the fence I might be able to find Colonel Hollows, give him Stanley's secret report and stories, and try to plead with him on Stanley's behalf. I walked along to the end of the crowd where it was just office girls who'd come down after work to see what all the fuss was about. There was a policeman standing guard at the gate there, a mountain of a man with a barrel chest and a bushy ginger moustache. I walked straight up to him and flashed the papers in front of him. I told him they were to be handed to the camp colonel from Tatura in person. He opened the gate a few inches, took the papers and started to leaf through them with his massive hands.

'I'm just the messenger,' I said. 'My brother-in-law's company is in charge of dismantling the camp. They're turning up all kinds of sensitive stuff.'

'I can't leave my post,' said the policeman.

'I can take them to him and come straight back,' I said. 'If you can tell me where he is.'

The policeman stared at the papers some more. He seemed particularly interested in the report and kept flipping the pages back and forth.

'The Japs had them hidden under the floorboards in the latrines,' I said. 'That's why they're a bit grubby.'

He snapped the report shut and handed the bundle back to me. Without a word, he pushed the gate open just wide enough for me to squeeze through.

'In the warehouse,' he said, gesturing to the long, low building behind him where about two hundred Japanese were lined up in rows, watched over by armed soldiers.

I made my way past a row of army transport trucks over to the nearest soldier and was about to tell him the same story as I'd told the policeman, when McMaster appeared in the entry to the warehouse. I waved to attract his attention and he waved back, signalling to the soldier to let me pass. McMaster motioned for me to join the line of women and children waiting alongside him. I pulled my felt hat down to hide my face, and on the order I shuffled along beside a mother and her small son, trying to appear as if I belonged to them. We were called to a halt about halfway across the deserted stretch of dock between the warehouse and the ship. About a hundred Japs were already standing there clutching their children and their meagre possessions.

McMaster grabbed hold of my elbow and dragged me back towards the warehouse. 'What the fuck are you playing at?' he said, keeping his voice down.

'I came to see Hollows.'

'What for?'

'Stanley doesn't want to go.'

He turned and glared at me fiercely. 'Don't be an idiot,' he said. 'He's got no bloody choice. You see those men?'

I glanced at the row of soldiers. Now that the dock was filling up with people they'd all raised their weapons and stood with them ready to fire.

'They're desperate for an excuse to shoot someone,' said McMaster.

I'd already attracted attention: an officer was approaching from the direction of the ship.

'Go home to your wife,' said McMaster, smiling now, making a show of shaking my hand.

On an impulse I ran towards the officer as if I had something urgent to tell him.

'Stop!' he shouted.

I stood breathless in front of him. 'Mechanic,' I said. 'Trouble with a vehicle.'

He hesitated. 'Where're your tools?'

'Left them in the truck.' I gestured at the transports.

He looked at the trucks, then at me. 'Piss off then.'

I tipped my hat, sprinted across the tarmac and climbed into the first vehicle I came to. From the driver's seat I could survey the whole dock. As far as I could tell, the loading had been in progress for some time because I could make out dozens of internees up on the deck of the ship, most of them men.

I thought if I could spot Stanley before he boarded I might be able to attract his attention. I envisaged spiriting him into the truck somehow and hiding him there until nightfall. But as hard as I looked I couldn't see him anywhere. When the sun went down, a row of weak lamps came on along the side of the warehouse then the *Daikai Maru*'s own dim lights came to life, making the wreck of a boat seem even more forlorn.

I watched as more and more people were herded out of the warehouse. They were made to line up in rows on the dock before they could proceed in single file to the gangway where a soldier shoved them one by one up onto the narrow boards that led to the lower deck of the ship.

All the time the shouting from the crowd behind the police barrier grew louder and angrier as more and more drunks spilled out of the dockside pubs, no doubt a few ex-servicemen among them. The yelling reached a crescendo when one of the Japs refused to set foot on the boards. I watched the soldier at the gate step towards him and pull out a pistol. Encouraged by the crowd, the soldier held the pistol to the man's head and started shouting at him to move.

That's when Colonel Hollows appeared. He marched from the warehouse straight over to the soldier, snatched the pistol out of his hand and shouldered him aside. The drunks disapproved. Hollows took the pistol over to the fence where they were gathered and aimed it straight at them. When they refused to quieten down he fired twice in the air above their heads. Then he marched back to the gangway and did something I'd never seen him do before. He bowed to the Jap who'd caused the problem, not once but two or three times, until eventually the man gave in and started to climb.

The man was halfway up the gangway when I saw his face for the first time. It was Shigeru, Stanley's uncle. He was looking up towards the deck to where Stanley, having appeared out of nowhere, was standing waiting, with both arms outstretched. His uncle waved to him almost casually, then in one swift movement he launched himself over the side ropes and dropped thirty feet into the water. Scarcely able to breathe now, I watched Stanley lean over the railings to see where his uncle had landed; and then it was only a matter of seconds before he threw himself after him.

When I recall Stanley's descent now it seems to take an agonisingly long time. He is standing on the top of the ship's railings in his patent leather shoes. He stretches his arms out wide. He takes a step into thin air, his suit jacket lifting like a cape at his back. He plummets down past the dismal lights and disappears into the shadows. I imagine that the instant before he hits the water he hears me yelling his name.

No one gave the order. One of the soldiers just started taking pot-shots into the water. I remember leaping out of the truck and taking a run at the marksman, then pushing him over the edge of the dock before diving in myself. After that I have trouble recollecting the exact order of events. I know the water was cold, and that it tasted of oil. I recall sinking as soon as my clothes were saturated: no matter how hard I struggled, my overalls conspired to twist around me and weigh my body down like a sack of stones. I thought of the kittens my father had drowned. I imagined them fighting to escape from their hessian sack and failing.

Stanley found me by accident, colliding with me as he circled around in search of his uncle. He even called me by his uncle's name as he hauled me out of the water. The last thing I remember was him crying like a baby as he was frogmarched away between two soldiers. When Stanley wouldn't stop wailing one of the soldiers raised his rifle and smashed the butt of it hard into the side of his head.

'That'll give you something to cry about ya Jap bastard,' said the soldier.

'Fuck you,' sobbed Stanley.

20

I told the police sergeant at King's Cross my name. 'I'm a reporter,' I said. 'I smuggled myself in to get a story.'

'Prove it,' he said.

'I would,' I said. 'Except that my wallet and notebook are at the bottom of the harbour.'

He kept me locked up in the cells for an hour and then he let me out because some more deserving customers showed up.

'Stay away from the docks,' he said. 'Or I won't be so nice the next time.'

I slept in my truck and the next morning at dawn I drove back to the wharf to watch Stanley's ship sail. I was just in time to see it vanish round the headland. Whether Stanley and his uncle were on board I had no way of knowing, but I waved anyway. And then I drove all the way to Watson's Bay to wait for the ship to come through the mouth of the harbour and head out to sea. When I could no longer make out the tiny speck on the ocean I left.

For three days I holed up in a pub in Darlinghurst and drank. On the fourth day I ran out of money and took to sleeping in my truck, and then, when I was too hungry to cling to my pride any longer, I rang my parents. They were living down on the Georges River by then, after my father had been transferred to the Sutherland Shire. The last time I'd seen them was Christmas 1944. I'd arrived home unannounced with a busted ankle and no uniform and my father had turned me away at the door. *You're no son of mine,* he said.

To my relief it was my mother who answered the phone.

'Where are you?' she said.

'Central Station. In the tearoom.'

'Thank God.' Her voice was so thin I could hardly hear her. 'Wait for me there.'

I waited two hours.

When she arrived she was flustered and nervy. 'I'm so sorry,' she said. 'I had to take three buses and a train. Your father thinks I'm at the pictures.'

She held me for a moment and that seemed to calm her.

'You're here now,' I said. 'That's the main thing.'

I was pleased to see her, but it wasn't a successful meeting. My mother cried the whole time and wouldn't eat her sandwiches.

'They're stale,' she said.

'They'll do me.' I wolfed them down. I'd already put away a plate of roast pork and vegetables but I was still hungry.

She didn't say much. She just sat in her chair by the window and stared at me while the tears rolled down her papery cheeks.

'I don't know what you want me to tell you,' I said. I was starting to think I'd made a mistake calling her. We had spoken twice in eighteen months and both times we'd argued.

'I'm sorry I didn't write to you.'

'So am I,' she said.

'I joined the army.'

'I thought you were dead.'

'I'm sorry.'

'You keep saying that.'

'Don't be like that,' I said. 'Let's just enjoy ourselves for a bit.'

I lit a smoke while she kept staring at me.

'You look awful,' she said.

'Thanks,' I said, turning my head away to blow smoke at the neighbouring table. There was a boy sitting there with his mother and father. He scowled at me then went back to reading his book.

'I got married,' I said. I didn't tell her about the baby because I couldn't. 'Her name's May. I met her at a dance.' I smiled at my mother and she frowned back.

'Where do you live?' she said.

'Melbourne. I drive trucks for my brother-in-law.'

'I thought you wanted to be an artist?'

'I wanted to be a lot of things.'

My mother brushed a few crumbs off the table then looked out the window again. 'I had a phone conversation with Bill,' she said. 'You remember Bill?'

My scalp tingled like someone had run their fingernails through my hair.

'He asked after you,' she said.

'What did you tell him?'

'I said we'd lost touch with you. I thought he might know where you were.'

'Why would he know where I was?'

'I thought all kinds of things, Arthur. You can't imagine.'

She poured herself some more tea even though it was cold by now.

'Does Dad ever talk about me?' I said.

Her face seemed to collapse internally, like a cake taken out of the oven too soon. She didn't say anything. It was like she'd lost the use of her tongue.

'It was his fault,' I said. 'He never understood me.'

I paused because I'd started to shake very slightly in the legs. It was a struggle not to sound like I was whining.

'He was jealous of you,' she said in her thin voice. 'From the moment you were born.'

'I know that,' I said. 'That's what makes it so fucking tragic.'

My mother stared down at the teacup in front of her where there was a dark skin forming on the top of her tea. 'I should have left,' she said.

'That's not what I meant.'

'It's true though. I should have walked out years ago.'

The most unsatisfactory thing about my mother was the way she always turned things around so that they were her fault, and invited you to blame her instead of the person who was responsible for the damage. This was the smokescreen my father had operated behind for years.

'Tell me about your wife,' she said, dabbing her eyes. 'You should have let me know you were getting married.'

'I know,' I said. 'It was a mistake. I knew you'd be worried.'

'Are you unhappy?'

The question was pointed. She wasn't asking out of idle curiosity. I could tell by the way she was looking straight at me that she expected the truth. I took a drag on my cigarette and stared out the window at the people milling about in the station. I envied them. They all had trains to catch and places to be while I sat marooned, my mother beside me, the past threatening to eviscerate the two of us in its huge maw.

'I've left her,' I said. 'I've run away.'

She stared hard at me then sighed.

'What?' I said. 'You asked if I was unhappy. I'm telling you.'

She waved to a waitress who was busy with another customer. As if this was the most important thing in the world to her right now, my mother made an elaborate show of taking the lid off the teapot and filling it with imaginary hot water.

'I'm going up north,' I said.

'To do what?'

'Start again.'

We sat in silence until the waitress arrived with the hot water, then we watched her pour it and replace the lid on the teapot. 'Will that be all?' she said.

'For the minute thank you,' said my mother. She slumped in her seat and put both hands up, cupping her cheeks with them.

She appeared to be holding her face on like a mask. After a minute or so she dropped her hands and drank her tea in silence while I smoked another cigarette.

'I never knew what to do with you,' she said finally.

'I know,' I said. 'I felt the same way.'

When it came time to go she opened up her purse and handed me a few fivers. I could see it was all the money she had apart from a few coins. I stood dumbly while she folded her arms around me and squeezed me tight.

'Don't be a stranger,' she said.

'Thanks, Mum,' I said.

I waved to her as she walked away, hoping she'd turn and see me but she didn't.

I wrote to May:

I'm going away for a while. Please direct my mail to Poste Restante at Brisbane GPO. Tell Ian I've sold the truck and there's a cheque for half the money in the post. I'll start paying the other half as soon as I can. Don't worry about me. I think this is the best thing for everyone. Take care of yourself and Stuart.
With love, Arthur

I boarded a train to Brisbane because I'd heard from the bloke who'd bought the truck that there were opportunities up north for someone interested in buying and selling ex-military vehicles. It wasn't a plan so much as an excuse not to go home, and that is how I imagined I would live my life from then on, finding one excuse after another.

And all the time I waited to hear from Stanley, the way you wait for a miracle to happen, for the dead to come alive again or for your enemies to turn. At first I waited in hope, half-expecting him to track me down and write to me from wherever he was to let me know he was all right. But as time went by and no letter came I waited without hope, which was easier.

21

I never spoke to anyone about Tatura. For many years I kept silent about everything that had happened there. If anyone asked me about my war I told them I'd been injured in a flying accident and had sat out the last few months of 1945 in a desk job. I avoided the company of men who'd fought the Japs, or been imprisoned by them. This seems less the case now, but for a long time after the war ended, men were still judged by what they had done or not done in the service of their country, and one's pride rested on this judgment. Needless to say, I wasn't proud in the least—of my service record, or of my private feelings. The war, as I recalled it, had done me nothing but harm.

May and Stuart were only the first casualties in what I think of as My Missing Years, starting in 1946 when I saw Stanley's ship sail away and ending when I met him again in 1963. If I relate a few salient events of that time it is only for the purpose of illustration. After the war my one and only aim became to distance myself from my previous life, whatever the cost. I took a variety of jobs, including a couple of seasons as a shearer, before finding a sales job with an engine-parts supplier back in Brisbane. I divorced May in 1947 in order to remarry. My second wife's name was Carol. She was a doctor's receptionist; I met her at the races on a Saturday and proposed to her on the Sunday. We divorced in 1952. After Carol there was Margaret, a schoolteacher with two little girls from a former marriage. We married in 1953 and divorced in 1956.

After Margaret I swore an oath I would never get married again no matter what because, try as I might, my heart was never in it. My wives, starting with May, had all said the same thing to me. *You're not here*, they said. *Even when you're here you're not here.* I told each of them I didn't know what they were talking about, but it was a lie. I knew exactly. They were talking about the way my climb up the company ladder consumed me, and the way I failed to take a real interest in anything else, including them. And they were talking about my coldness, which I'd tried to explain to them I could do nothing about. It was part of my constitution, I said. I wasn't a warm-blooded creature, except sometimes, after I'd had enough alcohol.

I rarely saw Stuart: I would drive down for Christmas every year to give him his presents and spend a desolate few hours at the Forbes house. But I was less comfortable in his company the older he grew. Stuart knew about Tatura because May had told him. Whenever we met up he wanted to know why I'd gone there instead of fighting on the front-line, and why I limped, and whether it was true the Japs cut off the heads of their own soldiers so they couldn't surrender, because that's what his uncle Ian had told him.

I said it was true but that the Japs had changed since the war.

'Changed how?' he said.

'They've modernised,' I said.

After he turned ten I decided he could fly up to Brisbane on Boxing Day instead of me driving all the way to Melbourne. And then I suggested he might like to come and visit me in his school holidays as well, because I found that I missed him when he wasn't there, and that phone calls only emphasised his absence.

In 1960, when a Japanese trade fair came to Brisbane I flew him up for the weekend so I could show him the gadgets and wizardry on show. It was also a way of impressing upon May, and her new husband Denis, that I was doing my best to be a good father.

May had reservations. 'What's the point of the exhibition?' she said. 'I suppose they're trying to sell us things.'

'How else are they going to rebuild their country?' I said. 'They're designing and manufacturing everything now, from sewing machines to high-speed trains, and we'd better wake up to them or we'll be consigned to the dust heap.'

'They have blood on their hands,' she said. The Forbes had never forgiven the Japanese for Owen's death. Like a lot of other people they were suspicious of anything made in Japan.

'You shouldn't generalise,' I said. 'There are good and bad Japs just like there are good and bad Australians.'

'They murdered millions of people,' she said.

'I'm sure they're very sorry.'

Stuart seemed to have grown a foot since the last time I'd seen him. When I shook his hand I realised, with a pang of regret, that we were eye to eye.

'How was the flight?' I said.

'Uneventful,' he said. At fourteen he had a highly developed sense of humour. It relied on this kind of unadorned statement of fact, delivered with perfect seriousness.

'No anti-aircraft fire from Moreton Bay on the way in?' I said.

'We caught them napping,' he said.

I drove him straight from the airport to Bretts Wharf where the *Aki Maru* was docked. On board was an exhibition of what the banners described as *Superior Creations by the Japanese Automotive Industry*. For half a day we wandered around from one booth to another while I instructed Stuart in the finer points of Japanese engine design. I explained how the Japanese had lost the war but were winning the peace, just like the Germans. 'It's sometimes an advantage to lose everything so you can sweep away the old and build something new,' I told him.

'Is that what you did?'

'What do you mean?'

'When you left Mum and me.'

We were in my car driving back from Bretts Wharf to New Farm. I lived there by myself in a house overlooking the Brisbane River. I glanced across at him and saw again how like his mother he was, pale and freckled. He was grinning the same way she grinned when she knew she'd said something unscripted.

'Did you miss me?' I said.

'You don't miss what you never had.'

He didn't mean it as a rebuke, and I was very grateful to him for that. So grateful that over a Chinese dinner in the Valley that evening I drank more than I should have and opened up to him about the camp and the kids I'd known there. I even talked about Stanley, but without going into detail.

'In another life,' I said, 'he would have been some kind of star. His name would have been up in lights somewhere.'

'What happened to him?'

'I have no idea. I presume he went back with all the others.'

'Why didn't you try to find him?'

I must have looked angry because Stuart seemed afraid to say any more.

'It wasn't just a matter of looking in the telephone book,' I said. My voice was shrill and I was immediately sorry.

In the car going home I apologised. 'It was such a strange part of my life,' I said. 'I think seeing all those people at the trade fair brought it all back to me.'

It was true. Outside of Chinatown it was rare to see an Asian face in Brisbane. To climb aboard the *Aki Maru* was to enter a floating microcosm of Japan. On deck we'd been greeted with smiles by a bevy of girls in uniform and men in suits who all reminded me of Stanley and his family. It was like hearing a piece of music again after a long time and remembering exactly where you were the first time you heard it and who you were with and what you said or failed to say to them.

'Mum says you never got over the war,' he said.

'That's rubbish,' I said. 'I did fine.'

Stuart went quiet after that and we drove without talking until we reached the house. Just as I turned into the driveway he turned and looked at me.

'Why did you keep getting married and divorced?'

'What kind of a question is that?'

'Just curious.'

I smiled to disguise my discomfort. 'I guess I'm an eternal optimist.'

'But you drew the line at more kids,' he said, sounding very like May.

'I'm not sure it was a deliberate decision.'

'It's a good thing. In my opinion.'

'Why's that?'

'Because I don't think you like them very much.'

I reached out and put my hand on his shoulder and patted him a couple of times because I didn't know what to tell him.

'Your mother knew what I was like when she married me,' I said in my own defence. 'I warned her.'

'So why did she marry you?'

'Why all the questions all of a sudden?' I said, attempting a smile.

Stuart glanced at me and turned away again.

I took my hand off his shoulder and waited for him to get out of the car, but he wasn't finished with me yet.

'She said you could have changed if you'd wanted to,' he said.

I laughed. 'Well she's wrong,' I said. 'I've spent years trying to change who I was, and it hasn't worked. I'm still the same person.'

I opened the car door and we went inside. Stuart got ready for bed while I sat in my study drinking. When I went to the guest room to check on him he was reading the program from the trade fair, but he put it down when I came to the door.

'You got everything you need?' I said.

'Yes thanks.'

'It's not true that I don't like kids.'

He looked at me steadily. 'Okay.'

'So now you know.'

He continued to stare at me. 'Why are you afraid to see Stanley again?'

'I didn't say I was afraid. I just said it wasn't that easy. I don't know what we'd have to talk about after all these years.'

Stuart picked up the trade-fair program again and started turning the pages.

'Just tell him how you feel,' he said in his matter-of-fact way. 'Tell him you've never forgotten him. Tell him he was the love of your life.'

I have to admit I was shocked. My impression was that he'd heard this from May, probably more than once, and that he didn't much care if it was true or not.

'Don't be ridiculous,' I said.

But I made a mistake. I should have sat down with him there and then and told him the facts. They are simple enough. I loved someone, then I lost him. It's a common story. I hear similar tales all the time.

I lingered in the doorway as if I expected an apology. Stuart closed the trade-fair program and put it on his bedside table.

'I found the exhibition very informative,' he said. 'Thank you for taking me.'

'I'm glad you enjoyed it.'

And then we wished each other goodnight and I left the room, wondering how I was going to put Stuart on the plane home in the morning without making a spectacle of myself.

22

McMaster found out where I was and wrote me a letter.

I've finally retired from my job in the Victorian Education Department and am enjoying a well-earned rest. Not that I'm idle for one moment. I recently returned from a trip to Japan where I had the most fascinating time. I managed to track down one or two of the families from Tatura and while my wife and I were in Tokyo they arranged a party for us. I've enclosed a photograph with the names of everyone on the back. They all remembered you very well and asked me to pass on their best wishes.

Stanley was not in the picture. When I called McMaster to thank him for his letter he told me nobody knew where Stanley was or what had become of his family.

'But I have feelers out,' he said. 'So I'll keep you posted.'

I heard nothing more for over a year. And then another letter arrived in the winter of 1963, this time with an address for Stanley's mother in Nagasaki. McMaster had spelled it out in Roman script for me. *Apparently,* he wrote, *the mother moved back to Nagasaki in about 1950, just before the Korean War, and Stanley definitely moved with her.*

Again I rang McMaster as soon as I received his letter.

'How do I get there?' I said.

'We went by ship,' said McMaster, 'But it's possible to fly.'

My thoughts were suddenly racing. I would have to tell my sales manager to run things for a couple of weeks and I'd have to get my housekeeper to look after the house and collect the mail, but aside from these considerations there was no reason why I couldn't go away, especially if I set up a few meetings with Japanese manufacturers in order to legitimise the expense.

McMaster asked me if I was still on the line.

'Yes,' I said. 'Thanks.'

'You won't be disappointed,' he said.

'What do you mean?'

'Tokyo has to be seen to be believed. It's like the war never happened.'

I thanked him again and rang off. Then I sat and stared at the address he'd written out for me, care of a company called *Chicago Night.* The name suggested that their business might have to do with the cousin in America. Either that or it was a brothel.

After I'd booked my flights I sent a note to Stanley's mother to say how pleased I was to have learned of her whereabouts.

I am hoping to get in touch with Stanley as well. You may remember that we were quite friendly in the camp but I've had no news of him since then. Please give him my best wishes.
Yours sincerely,
Arthur Wheeler.

I telephoned May to tell her I'd be away for the school holidays, so I wouldn't be able to take Stuart as planned.

'Tell him yourself,' she said. She didn't sound very surprised. It was as if she'd been waiting for me to let Stuart down. I could imagine Denis in the background mouthing, *I told you so.*

I waited while Stuart came to the phone. A thousand miles from where he was lifting himself out of his chair or coming in reluctantly from the garden, I pictured my son the way he'd looked the first time I'd seen him, how his little face had seemed so worried. And it occurred to me that my most consistent emotion, the sentiment that had governed my life, was grief.

'I'm taking your advice,' I said.

'What did I say?' he said. 'I can't remember.'

'I'm going to see if I can track down that boy I told you about. The one I knew in the camp.'

Stuart was only half-listening. He kept talking to May at the same time as he was talking to me.

'Mum says to ask you to bring me back a transistor radio.'

'It's on my list.'

He handed the phone back to May and I told her about McMaster's two letters.

'Where's Nagasaki?' she said.

'They dropped the bomb on it,' I said.

'I know *that*. But where is it in relation to Tokyo.'

'Two days on the train. Going west. It's on the island of Kyushu. Actually it's nearer to Korea than it is to Tokyo.' I remembered the time Stanley had shown me Nagasaki on the map in the schoolboy history book from Matron Conlon's library. I pictured his slender hand resting on the page.

May said she had to go out and wished me a safe trip. 'I hope you find what you're looking for,' she said.

'So do I.'

There was a pause and then she said, 'I think we made a mistake getting married when we did. I didn't think so at the time but I think so now. It was my fault. I'm sorry.'

I told her I didn't think it was anybody's fault.

'You tried to warn me,' she said.

'I didn't try hard enough,' I said. 'I was so confused back then. I didn't know if I was Arthur or Martha.'

Which made her laugh. 'That's funny,' she said.

'It wasn't at the time,' I said.

She laughed some more and her high spirits emboldened me, finally, to tell her I was sorry that I'd run out on her when I did and how I'd always regretted it.

'I haven't forgiven you,' she said. 'I don't think I ever will.'

'I don't blame you,' I said. And I meant it.

'Don't forget Stuart's transistor,' she said. 'And bring me back some silk.'

'How much?'

'As much as you can carry.'

23

I spent my first two days in Japan touring motor showrooms in Tokyo with an interpreter I'd booked through my travel agent. Her name was Hiroko and she'd lived in America, first as a student, which I gathered was unusual for a girl, then as a secretary in a bank.

'Why did you come back to Japan?' I asked her.

'To find a husband,' she said smiling. Whenever she smiled she covered her mouth with her hand so I couldn't see her teeth.

'Were you successful?' We were in the lobby of my hotel, waiting for a taxi to take me to Tokyo station so I could catch the train for Kyushu.

'I'm still looking.'

'What kind of men do you like?'

'Actually I don't like Japanese men,' she said. 'They never say what they think, unless they're drunk.'

I'd seen them in the hole-in-the-wall bars near my hotel, businessmen dressed in identical suits, sitting in rowdy groups and filling up the tiny spaces with their noise and smoke.

'What about Americans?' I said.

'Americans tell you everything,' she said. 'I like that better. But my parents want me to marry a good Japanese boy. What about in Australia?'

'We talk a lot,' I said. 'But it's mostly bullshit.'

She started to look in her dictionary but I told her she wouldn't find it there, and I explained the meaning.

'Oh you mean horseshit,' she said, which made me laugh because she pronounced it the same way Stanley did, the emphasis on the second syllable.

'For instance,' I said. 'I told my company I'm here to look at cars.'

She looked confused until I explained that the man I'd asked her to track down in Nagasaki was not in the motor-car business but was someone I'd met in Australia during the war.

'I see,' she said.

'The last time I saw my friend was in 1946.'

Hiroko didn't respond. She didn't like to talk about the war. All she would say was that it was a very sad time but now was much better. She liked to point out that the Olympic Games next year would make Tokyo into a modern city just like London or New York.

'Does your father talk about the war?' I said.

'Never.'

'Don't you ask him questions?'

'No.'

The taxi arrived and Hiroko helped me load my bags in the boot and then bowed to me while I climbed in the back. She had wanted to come to help me buy my ticket but I'd decided to see if I could remember any of the basic Japanese I'd picked up in the camp. As a precaution she'd written everything down so I could show it to the ticket office if I got stuck. She told the taxi driver where to take me, then stood on the curb bowing until we were deep in the Tokyo traffic and I lost sight of her.

While we cruised across town I thought about what she'd said, that Tokyo was turning into London or New York. I'd never been to either place but it struck me that Tokyo was like a Western city only in the most superficial way, that you just had to leave the main streets and venture into the laneways and back alleys, as I'd done on my two nights alone in the city, to feel like you'd left everything familiar behind. The sights and sounds and smells were not like anything I'd ever experienced before. I wasn't exactly afraid on my night walks, but I wasn't entirely comfortable either. I hardly ever saw another foreigner, for instance, and this made me nervous, in the same way I'd been nervous when I'd first arrived at Tatura, and I found myself feeling outnumbered the way I had back then. Not that anyone seemed hostile in the least. They stared, but it seemed like simple curiosity. And of course I stared back, searching every face for similarities to the faces I'd known so well in the camp, seeing resemblances in the eyes, the noses, the cheekbones, the glossy hair.

And then there were the boys. Stanley would be thirty-three by now, I knew that, but the schoolboys I passed in the street reminded me of the way he'd looked when I'd first met him. Especially the bigger ones who were no longer children. I sought them out in the shops and in the trains, waiting for that look they had—the look that said they were somewhere in between childhood and adulthood, savouring their own thoughts, savage the way Stanley had been, liable to believe absolutely in some future they could see up ahead of them as bright as day, but couldn't catch.

In Tokyo it had taken Hiroko hours to find the telephone number for *Chicago Night*. She'd called to say I was coming and written the number down alongside the address in Japanese in my diary. She'd also trained me to say *chikago naito* so that I'd be understood if I needed to ask directions.

'Did you ask him about Stanley?' I dared to ask.

'He was busy,' she said.

I wasn't sure if that meant she hadn't asked, or if she'd asked and the man had been too busy to answer. Not that it made much difference now. At least the owner knew I was on my way. I'd asked Hiroko to tell him the name of my hotel in Nagasaki in case he wanted to leave me a message, or better still if he wanted to let Stanley know where I was staying. I half-expected Stanley to be waiting for me there when I arrived.

The possibility that Stanley didn't want to see me hadn't occurred to me. At least it had, but I'd rejected the idea out of hand. At that stage I was still vain enough to think that once I arrived on Stanley's doorstep he would naturally welcome me like a long-lost brother. I even dared to imagine other feelings he might still have for me as well.

Hiroko had warned me about the rain. She'd said the tail of a typhoon was passing over Kyushu and the weather was likely to be very wet. When I changed trains in Hakata the rain outside the station was torrential, and then all the way to Nagasaki I stared out the window at a grey world of water and fog that was like the inside of a cloud.

I'd seen pictures of Hiroshima and Nagasaki after the bombs had been dropped. The cities had been reduced to moonscapes. It didn't seem possible that in such a short time a new city had been built out of the ruins, with train stations and trams and hotels and department stores that were full of people. As we pulled into town I wondered where they'd all come from and why they looked the same as any other rain-soaked crowd, umbrellas up, raincoats flapping. I suppose I'd expected to find a city still on its knees and a population of survivors still visibly suffering the after-effects of the bomb. What I hadn't imagined was this pretty seaside town with mist-shrouded green hills spilling down towards the bay, and a harbour full of shipping. It was as if nothing more violent than the weather had ever happened here.

I handed the taxi driver the address of my hotel and we drove ten minutes along the harbour-front then up a winding tree-lined backstreet that was a jumble of apartment buildings, noodle shops and grocers. I'd asked Hiroko to book me into a Japanese-style hotel and she'd found the Seibold Ryokan, named, I later learned from the hotel brochure, after a famous German who'd taught

Western medicine to the Japanese and made pioneering studies of its flora and fauna. When the taxi stopped I saw that the hotel boasted a garden at the front enclosed by an elegant fence the colour of wheat.

My room was on the ground floor and overlooked the garden. A woman brought me green tea and showed me how to prepare it. After she withdrew I lay back on the tatami floor to rest. In a few minutes I'd dozed off into a half-sleep in which I knew I was dreaming and was afraid of waking up before the dream was over. Stanley was in the dream, but only vaguely. He was on board the same train as I was but he was in another carriage so I wasn't able to sit with him. When I asked the conductor if I could change seats and move to Stanley's carriage he said no. And so for the whole journey I was worried that Stanley might not know I was aboard or might get out at a station without telling me and leave me alone on the train.

When I woke up it was dark and muggy and I was covered in sweat. I took a shower as best I could in the narrow bathroom, then dressed and went to the front desk to ask for directions to *chikago naito*. I showed the desk clerk the address Hiroko had written down.

'Taxi?' he said.

'Can I walk? Is it far?'

'Rain,' he said. 'Taxi.' He reminded me of the conductor in my dream. He had the same way of preventing me, very politely, from doing what I wanted to do.

I waited outside for the taxi, under a borrowed umbrella. I hadn't been permitted to leave the premises without it. The rain had eased a little but it was still wet and, when I looked up at the streetlights, I could see the raindrops lined up in mid-air, not falling but moving left to right like bees swarming.

The taxi driver dropped me at the end of a street too narrow and packed with pedestrians for him to navigate. He bobbed his head up and down and apologised, *sumimasen, sumimasen*, then opened my door with the lever he had next to his seat. I paid and stepped out into the rain while he pointed in the direction I should go. *Chikago naito. Migi no hou.*

'*Arigato*,' I said. 'Thank you.'

He waved and drove off slowly.

I entered a warren of restaurants and bars and nightclubs, with neon signs out the front and touts trying to entice the passers-by to come inside. I wasn't the only foreigner there. I passed some American boys, obviously sailors on shore leave, wandering along in pairs trying to keep their eyes off the photographs of dancing girls and topless waitresses that the touts kept flashing at them. *Hey American*, the touts called out. *How are you? Beri weru san kyuu.*

Chicago Night was at the end of the lane and up a steep stone stairway. I saw the sign from the bottom of the steps, written in English. I didn't think it could be a brothel, although it seemed to be surrounded by them. There were no pictures of girls, no touts, just an elegant black-framed gate, which led to an irregular stone pathway dotted here and there with lanterns. I felt a thrill as I entered, as if I'd found a portal to another world, an Alice-in-Wonderland rabbit hole. At the end of the pathway was another gate, this time a wooden sliding door. Beyond this gate was a curtain, and behind the curtain was a room about half the size of an average living room. It didn't take long to see that Stanley wasn't there. Apart from the barman and his single customer the place was deserted. They both looked up at me and chorused a greeting I didn't understand.

'*Konban wa*,' I replied. It was hard to be heard over the music, an old-fashioned jazz number I knew because Bill had liked to sing it to me. *You always hurt the one you love, the one you shouldn't hurt at all.*

I sat down on a stool at the counter, next to a young man of about nineteen or twenty dressed in a loud Hawaiian shirt. The counter ran down the centre of the room and divided it in half again. I pointed to the bottle of Scotch whisky that was on display on a shelf behind the bar, along with a whole range of other foreign and Japanese drinks. The wall and the ceiling above the shelf were decorated with album covers and posters of American jazz greats. The barman asked me in English how I wanted my drink.

'Ice and soda,' I said.

Wakarimasita. I presumed this meant he understood, since he turned the volume down on the record player and started to prepare my drink with an unusual amount of care.

'My name is Arthur Wheeler,' I said. 'I'm looking for Ueno Saburo-san.' This was another thing Hiroko had made me practise, how to pronounce Stanley's real name.

The barman merely nodded. He was a man of around fifty with greying hair cropped close to his scalp and a neat salt-and-pepper moustache. His wire glasses gave him an incongruously learned look, as if his daytime job was at a university and the bar was just a hobby.

'Actually I'm looking for his mother, Mariko-san,' I said.

He placed my drink on the counter and added a plastic stick to stir it with. Beside it he placed a small plate of green edamame beans.

'Yes,' he said, and then turned to the young man. 'This is my friend Haruo.'

I shook hands with Haruo, who apparently spoke no English. He smiled broadly and ducked his head.

'My name is Ikeda,' said the barman.

I shook his hand then removed the plastic stirrer from my glass and took a sip of my drink.

'From Australia?' said Ikeda-san.

I nodded.

Ikeda-san wiped the counter with a cloth and said something to Haruo, at which Haruo jumped up off his stool and trotted towards a back door hidden behind a curtain. He gave me a little duck of the head before he disappeared.

Ikeda-san placed another dish on the counter.

'*Daikon,*' he said. 'Please try.'

He handed me some chopsticks and watched while I chewed. It was some vegetable I couldn't identify chopped into matchsticks and massaged with a sweet vinegary dressing.

'Good,' I said. '*Oishii.*'

He bowed in a womanish way.

'Do you know Saburo-san?' I said.

He didn't reply. I couldn't tell if I'd made him uncomfortable or not. He attended to a dish he was preparing on a narrow bench underneath the counter. The cooking arrangements, like everything else in the bar, were cramped but functional.

He looked up from his work. 'I'm sorry,' he said. 'Please wait a minute.'

I waited for half an hour, drinking steadily, eating everything Ikeda-san put in front of me. Nobody else came into the bar.

'It's quiet,' I said.

'Too early,' he said.

'Have you owned the bar for long?'

'I don't own the bar. I only work here. It started 1951.'

'I was very surprised when I arrived in Nagasaki. So many new buildings.'

'Yes. Everything new.' He didn't seem convinced that this was a good thing. 'When I came back here there was nothing,' he said. 'No house, no family, no work.'

'Where were you?' I said. 'Before that.'

'China.'

After a long silence he asked me if I would like to hear another record.

'Yes please.'

'You choose.'

I told him he could choose because I didn't know a lot about music and he seemed to know a great deal.

'You like Ink Spots?' he said.

'I had a friend who liked them very much,' I said.

He went to a long cupboard in the corner and opened the sliding doors. Inside were shelves packed tight with hundreds of records. He searched for a minute then pulled one out. He showed me the cover. Ella Fitzgerald and The Ink Spots.

'That's a big collection,' I said.

'We buy from America,' he said. 'Chicago.'

'*Chikago naito*,' I said, and he laughed.

'Yes yes, *chikago naito*. Your Japanese very good.'

He was just taking the record out of its sleeve when the door swung open and Haruo came in followed by a woman in her mid-fifties wearing a lolly-pink kimono and a short perm. Stanley's mother had changed. I'd never spoken to her at Tatura but I'd seen her often enough and I'd heard her on the night she'd attempted to poison herself. That dishevelled, unruly woman had gone. In her place was a trim, pretty hostess with a direct gaze and a professional smile.

'Welcome,' she said. 'Good evening. So happy you come.'

Her dental work flashed gold under the counter lights.

I realised when I stood up that I'd had too much to drink. The room rolled a little as if we were on the water.

'Hello,' I said. I held out my hand and then checked myself and bowed instead. Stanley's mother bowed back.

'You Wheeler-san,' she said. 'I know you anywhere.' She was flirting with me, but it was more of a reflex than a sign of affection.

'Thank you,' I said.

It was either the shock of seeing her again or the drink, but I felt like my legs were about to give way underneath me. I sat down on my stool again and held the counter to stop myself from losing my balance.

242

'I'm sorry,' I said. 'Too much whisky.'

Stanley's mother said something to Ikeda-san in Japanese and the next thing there was a glass of water on the counter in front of me. I drank the whole thing down.

'I came to see Stanley,' I said. 'Saburo-san.'

'He isn't here,' said his mother, her smile fixed.

She went around to the other side of the bar and helped herself to a drink from a giant bottle of sake. Then she said something to Haruo and he went to lock the front door.

I had a terrible feeling that I'd done the wrong thing by coming here and I apologised again.

'I don't want to cause any trouble,' I said.

'No trouble,' she said.

Haruo and Ikeda-san exchanged a look and then Ikeda-san offered me a cigarette from a pack he kept on the counter. Stanley's mother took one too and Haruo lit first mine and then hers. She took a long, slow draw and stared at me over the top of her glass. I remembered the wild look she'd sometimes given me on the parade ground at Tatura. That was gone now. Where she'd once looked fearful she now appeared indifferent, lazy almost, as if everything that could have happened had happened and there was nothing left to be afraid of.

'Away on business,' she said.

'What sort of business does Stanley do now?' I asked.

She looked at Ikeda-san.

'Real estate,' he said. '*Fudosan.*'

'When will he be back?' I said. 'I've come a very long way and I don't have a lot of time. I have meetings in Tokyo.'

'Tomorrow,' said Stanley's mother. 'We go tomorrow. Where you stay?'

I gave her one of the hotel cards I'd brought with me in case I got lost.

'I come there,' she said. 'Twelve o'clock.'

I thanked her again and then she suggested we get something to eat.

'You like *gyoza*?' she said. 'Dumplings?'

'I'm not sure,' I said, 'but I'm not that hungry after all the food Ikeda-san has given me to eat.' I smiled at him and took out my wallet to pay, but she waved it away.

I offered money to Ikeda-san, but he refused to even look at it. *Dame, dame.*

Haruo came with me to the front gate and showed me out. Stanley's mother was already walking away up the street, a small, determined figure. Her umbrella was the same loud pink as her kimono. I bowed to Haruo and said goodbye, then hurried away after her.

24

Stanley's mother took me to a place not far from the bar where she was obviously well known. She introduced me at length, to the cooks, to the customers, to the girl who served us our beer and dumplings. Nobody here spoke English, so all I could do was sit on my stool and smile whenever I heard my name mentioned.

Along with the dumplings came two bowls of steaming noodles. Stanley's mother showed me how to suck them up without burning my mouth on the hot soup and then we concentrated on eating for the ten minutes it took to finish off a bowl. All the time I was wondering what she thought about my showing up like an apparition. Apart from an occasional sideways glance, she barely looked at me. I might have been a child she'd been conned into taking care of for the evening while his parents were out enjoying themselves.

'Very good,' I said, drinking the dregs of my soup from the bottom of the bowl the way Mariko-san had done.

'Thank you very much,' she said, which made me wonder whether the dumpling shop was hers, as well as the bar, since she seemed so at home in both.

'Is Ikeda-san your husband?' I ventured.

She laughed for the first time all evening, waving her hand in front of her face as if she was swatting a fly. *Chigau, chigau. Bad joke.*

'Is Saburo-san married?' I said. It was a possibility. In all the years I'd waited for news of him, I'd tried to imagine a life for Stanley, a pretty wife, a few handsome children, success in some profession or other that required a perfect command of English.

Mariko-san shook her head. *Mada desu.* Not yet.

Later, when we were walking again out in the busy alleyway, she turned to me and asked me if I was married.

'Divorced,' I said.

'Children?'

'One boy.'

'Me too,' she said, giggling. 'Divorced. One boy.' She slapped me on the arm coquettishly.

I was still drunk. The thought of meeting Stanley again sent a surge of warmth through me, starting at my knees and reaching all the way to the back of my eyes. I thought I was going to cry.

'It's very strange,' I said. 'The last time I saw Stanley was at the ship. The soldiers shoot. Bang bang. He jump in the water.'

It must have been the wrong thing to say because Mariko-san quickened her pace and I had to hurry to keep up with her. At the end of the alleyway we came to a wider road where a line of taxis was parked. She waved to the driver of the first one and he swung around to where we were standing.

'*Oyasumi*,' she said. 'Goodnight.'

'*Oyasumi*,' I said. 'I'll see you tomorrow. Thank you for dinner.'

And as soon as I was in the taxi she scuttled away as if she was pleased to be rid of me.

I slept badly and woke with a headache. When I opened the curtains the sun streamed into the room making the dust motes swirl and circle like sparks. I slid the windows open and sat on the narrow verandah overlooking the garden, breathing in the fragrance of pine sap and moss. I daydreamed about the possibility of staying in Japan for a while longer. There was so much here that appealed to me for reasons I would never fathom in a week. And of course there was my craving for Stanley, undiminished after all these years. As soon as I'd landed in Tokyo I'd felt a redoubled longing to be near him, to be his favoured companion.

I showered and dressed, trembling with terror at what the day held in store. My biggest fear was that I might be an embarrassment to Stanley after all this time. I already suspected that his mother disapproved of my visit, that she'd been forced to play the go-between against her better judgment. In the meantime I had three hours to fill in before our twelve o'clock meeting.

I packed my bags and went to the front desk to check out.

'You leave?' said the desk clerk.

'Five-fifteen train,' I said.

I glanced at my watch. It was just past nine.

I explained to the desk clerk that I planned to take my bags with me to lunch and head to the station from there.

'Lunch?' he said. 'Now?'

'No. Twelve o'clock. Now I walk.'

'Hot. Many hills. You drive.'

It seemed useless to argue with him.

Within ten minutes he was waving me off in a taxi.

'Back here twelve o'clock,' I said to the driver. I leaned forward and showed him on my watch-face, then I held up one finger on one hand and two fingers on the other. He nodded and said nothing.

We drove in silence through the city, down to the harbour, up the slopes where the churches were and all the time I fretted and fidgeted like an over-anxious kid on his way to an exam. Two or three times the driver stopped the car so I get could out and walk around, but I never took him up on the suggestion. I remained in my seat and pointed at my watch to indicate we were on a schedule. At the A-bomb memorial I finally agreed to leave the car. I spent an hour inside and came out so troubled and confused that I decided to pay off the driver and walk back along the main road to the hotel. It started to rain again, not that I really noticed. It was as if my thoughts had jammed from seeing all the photographs of shadow people, and the bits of twisted, melted objects in glass cases, the scorched clothing.

Stanley's mother was waiting for me when I returned. She and the desk clerk were standing in the lobby beside my bags. They both bowed as I walked in and then the desk clerk offered me a handtowel to dry my jacket and my hair. Out in the street a long white Cadillac sat with its engine running. Stanley's mother took charge, bundling me inside the car and supervising the desk clerk while he loaded my luggage into the boot. She lowered her umbrella and climbed in after me, settling herself on the leather seat in a huffy kind of way, as if I'd somehow ruined her morning.

'I'm sorry,' I said. I wasn't sure why I was apologising, except that now she seemed to command deference. I'd noticed it the night before in the noodle shop, where we were served ahead of customers who'd been there before we came in.

When she didn't reply I sat back in my deep seat and surveyed the car's luxurious interior. I'd never ridden in a Cadillac before. I wasn't prepared for the queasy sensation of floating along above the road, only coming into contact with it again when we slowed down at corners or pulled up at lights. My tremors from the morning returned and I was fearful I might faint or be sick. My headache hadn't left me either. I could feel it in my teeth. I remembered back to my first wedding, how I'd been so paralysed with nerves I'd failed to remember my lines and had to be prompted. *I do.* How ridiculous I must have seemed back then, and here I was again, as giddy as a bride. I didn't bother asking where we were going. I just sat and listened to the hum of the engine, which seemed to be coming from a long way off.

Stanley's mother left me at the front door of the restaurant, delivering me there like a parcel. Out on the footpath she handed me over to a waiter who was expecting me. Wet and not remotely hungry, I followed him up some stairs and into a private room where Stanley was waiting for me. I knew him immediately, of course, the same feline head, the same golden eyes with their shards of green. His skin had coarsened a little and his hair had lost some of its lustre, but apart from that he was unchanged.

'Arthur,' he said, his voice setting off a fit of the shakes in my knees. 'Come.'

He was standing by the window, surveying the rain-soaked town as if he owned it. In his sky-blue suit and gold-rimmed glasses he looked like a pimp.

'It's better at night,' he said.

And then he put his arm around my shoulder and I smelled the Camel cigarettes on his breath and it was like I'd come home after a journey lasting years.

'What are you doing here?' he said.

'I hardly know,' I said.

He gave me a choice of drinks, indicating the bottles on the table. 'Beer, whisky, or the local vodka?'

'Whatever you're having.'

'All three then.'

He gestured for me to sit down at the table.

'We're having a Nagasaki-style lunch,' he explained, sounding like a tour guide. 'The most famous local dish is *Nagasaki champon*.'

He poured two beers then sat down opposite me.

'I'll drink to that,' I said, lifting my glass. 'Whatever it is.'

Stanley noticed my trembling hand and smiled. 'It's not Japanese or Chinese or Portuguese,' he said, 'It's all three mixed up. A trader's dish.'

'Is that what you do? Trade?'

I gestured to the lavish table-setting and the private room and the view.

'I do many things,' he said, launching into a long speech about how he was riding a wave, how the future belonged to Asia because the West was all about *might is right* while the East was about *gaman*, which I knew meant some special blend of patience and endurance.

'I want to invite you to the Olympics next year,' he said. 'The whole world will come and see how we've lifted this country out of the rubble.'

There was something strained in the way he talked, as if his sole aim was to impress me with his rise in the world. He hadn't actually looked at me since I'd entered the room.

'Thank you,' I said. 'Do I call you Saburo now, or Stanley?'

'Either. To my American friends I'm Stanley, to the rest I'm Saburo.'

I watched him gulp down his beer and stare forlornly into his empty glass. And then he looked up at me at last and I saw how tired he was, not just in a physical sense, but in some permanent way, as if he'd seen too much of life before he was ready.

'How did you find me?' he said.

'McMaster tracked you down.'

'I never expected to see you again,' he said, sounding almost angry.

He took a pair of clean glasses and poured us each a shot of Japanese liquor out of a stoneware jar. At that moment a waiter appeared with two steaming dishes of noodles in soup and placed them in front of us.

After the waiter left the room Stanley watched me sip my drink. It burned as it went down.

'How long can you stay?' he said.

'I leave this afternoon.'

'Pity. I wanted to show you around.'

'I did a tour this morning. I went to the A-bomb memorial.'

Stanley nodded. 'What did you think?'

'I don't know exactly. Sad.'

He smiled at me. 'You were born sad, Arthur.'

He picked up his chopsticks and started to eat noisily. I did the same. The noodles were thick and served in a creamy soup made from vegetables and fresh seafood.

'Very good,' I said.

Stanley said nothing. He poured us some more liquor and we drank.

'What happened to your uncle?' I said.

Stanley was quiet for a moment as if he was trying to decide how much to tell me, given that I knew nothing.

'He died on the boat,' he said. 'The crew were stealing our rations and he complained.'

'I'm sorry I couldn't save you,' I said. 'I did try. That's what I was doing on the docks that day.'

Stanley looked at me across the table and laughed.

'What's so funny?' I said.

'You talk like a boy scout.'

There was a hint of the old mockery in his voice, which made me strangely gleeful. It was a sign that at least I still had the power to irritate him.

He finished his lunch and wiped his mouth on his serviette. Then he felt in his pocket and found his cigarettes. I watched him light one, then toss the packet in my direction like we were still teenagers.

'So how do you like my restaurant?' he said, holding his breath momentarily then exhaling with extra force.

'Not bad,' I said, laughing. 'I should have guessed.'

'I own seven bars and three restaurants. Not bad for a kid who arrived here with nothing but a suitcase and a mad mother.'

'Your mother seems fine now.'

'She is. We're all fine.'

'And your father?'

'The last time I heard he was in South America,' he said.

He pushed his hair back off his forehead with the gesture I remembered from Tatura. My heart fluttered like a startled bird.

'So what do you want to do after lunch?' he said.

'I don't really have a plan,' I said. 'If you're busy just say so.'

He slowly raised himself out of his chair and went to stand by the window again with his back to me. For a moment he swayed as if he'd had a blow to the head, then he put his hand on the sill to steady himself.

'Are you in Japan for your work?' he said.

'Yes. I buy and sell engine parts.'

There was a silence after that. I put my chopsticks down and left my lunch unfinished.

'You shouldn't have come,' he said, turning around. He leaned back, resting his head on the glass.

'Why not?' I said.

He stared at me, looking less than friendly. I could tell he'd stopped enjoying himself. I don't mean that afternoon but, at some point in the past, things had ceased to please him. I wanted to think it was at around the same time as I'd left Tatura and abandoned him, although far worse things had no doubt happened to him since.

'I wanted to see you,' I said.

'What for?' he said, surprised.

I paused for a moment, as if I wasn't sure where to start.

'I wanted a re-match,' I said.

I'd hoped to make him laugh but instead he suddenly appeared to deflate, like a balloon with a slow leak, and all of his puffed-up pride seemed to desert him. He walked towards me and stopped when he reached the back of my chair. The next moment I felt his hand on my shoulder, then the back of his fingers on the base of my neck at my hairline. It was only for an instant but it was enough to send all of my senses rushing to the spot like starved things.

'I have something for you,' he said. He was sitting down again by then. He reached inside his jacket and pulled out a small package. 'Open it when you're on the train.'

He pushed the package across the table towards me. I picked it up and shook it to see if it rattled.

Stanley was not amused. 'Would you like to see my latest project?'

'Depends what it is,' I said, slipping the package into my pocket.

'I'm building a Western-style restaurant,' he said. 'Down near Dejima.'

'Where the foreign traders lived,' I said. I'd read about Dejima in the hotel brochure.

'You've been doing your homework.'

'I'm interested.'

'Arthur the schoolteacher.'

I asked him if he still liked to write.

He shook his head. 'No time.' He stared down at his hands and sighed. 'You always had the wrong idea about me Arthur.'

'What do you mean?'

'You always thought I was good.'

'You were,' I said. 'You were the best, bravest person I ever knew.' I blushed. This was the nearest I'd ever been to declaring my love for him. A better man would have rushed to Stanley and embraced him at that moment, but I sat numbly in my chair and stared at the floor.

'You should forget about the past,' he said. 'None of it matters any more.'

The waiter reappeared at the door and bowed. Stanley broke off and said something to him in Japanese, after which the waiter started to clear away our glasses and drinks.

I excused myself and went to the bathroom. I stared at myself in the oval-shaped mirror and tried to understand what had just taken place. It had only been a gesture, that hand on the back of my neck, but immediately I was seventeen again and Stanley was leaning over to kiss me in Matron Conlon's infirmary. I stood before the mirror and raised my hands to my flushed face.

My skin seemed to be giving off waves of heat. Of course it was the drinking I'd done all through lunch to steady my nerves, but there was also was a wild hopefulness I hadn't experienced since my youth.

Naturally it couldn't last. By the time we were back in the car Stanley's mood had soured. I wasn't sure if he'd decided not to like me again, or if it was something his driver had said. They'd argued briefly after we'd set out from the restaurant. Now both of them sat sulking while the Cadillac ferried us, almost independently it seemed, across the darkening town.

The driver waited in the car while Stanley and I wandered around outside the new restaurant and watched the carpenters at work. We crossed the road to Dejima, trying to dodge the rain. There wasn't much to see, just a tiny area in between two major roads, where a couple of big wooden, barn-like structures had been erected to house the exhibits. Inside there was little logic to the exhibition and very few English signs. Stanley did not even pretend to be interested until we reached the last glass case, which contained a scroll painting of the design for Dejima with all of its modest dimensions duly noted.

'This land is worth a small fortune,' he said. 'It's a wonder they haven't built a department store on it.'

'Why did they lock the foreigners away here?' I said. 'What were they scared of?'

'The same reason they locked us away,' said Stanley. It was the first time he'd referred to Tatura directly in the whole time we'd been together. 'Fear, suspicion, ignorance.'

It occurred to me then that this might be the cause of

his anger: that my coming here to see him had stirred up all kinds of resentment and regret.

'I thought you'd forgotten the past,' I said, trying to humour him or, failing that, to provoke another unguarded moment, a glance or a smile that would tell me I was forgiven. But Stanley just walked out ahead of me into the rain without saying another word and I came to the unspeakably desolate conclusion that I had made a fool of myself showing up here, that Stanley was not going to offer me any of the consolation I was seeking.

Once we were back in the car he suggested we stop on the way to the station for a last drink at *chikago naito*.

'One for the road,' he said.

'I'm already drunk.'

'Not drunk enough,' he said. 'You can't leave Kyushu until you've tasted *imojochu* from Miyazaki.'

And so we went to the bar and stayed for forty minutes listening to Miles Davis. At least I stayed there, while Stanley went off to take a phone call and came back just in time to drive me to the station. While I waited, Mr Ikeda poured me drinks and politely answered all my questions about Stanley without telling me very much at all.

'Is he happy?' I said.

'Yes,' said Mr Ikeda. 'Very happy.'

'Why didn't he marry?' I said, not expecting an honest reply.

'Too busy working. And you? Are you happy?' He smiled at me kindly.

'I am now. Now that I've seen my friend again.' At which my eyes filled up with stupid tears and I had to wipe them away while

Mr Ikeda stared down at his hands and pretended not to notice.

Stanley came with me onto the platform, leaving the driver down in the car park with the Cadillac. He even carried my suitcase for me.

'You don't have to wait,' I said. 'I know you're busy.'

But he ignored me and we sat down together on a bench under cover and watched the rain troop across the platform in ghostly squadrons.

'Look at them all,' he said, gesturing at the passengers waiting on the platform. 'Like mental patients. No idea where they've been, no idea where they're going.'

I laughed.

'You think I'm joking?' he said. 'Why did you always think I was joking?'

'That's not true. I took everything you said very seriously. I even memorised your best lines.'

'Like what? What did I say?'

'That any man who doesn't know the difference between a curveball and a slider doesn't deserve to live,' I said, in the best version of his accent that I could manage.

'You remember that?'

'Like it was yesterday. The past has a hold over me I can't explain. That's why I'm here. I never forgot you. Not for a single day. I wanted you to know that.' I stopped and stared at him.

He took hold of my hand and squeezed hard on it. 'Poor Arthur.'

We sat like that for ten minutes while a few people openly

stared at us and others cast furtive glances in our direction. When Stanley could tolerate it no longer he shouted something at the old lady standing closest to us and she scuttled away. After that nobody looked at us again until Stanley stood up. He bowed to me twice, very low, making noises about needing to get back to work and, before I could stand up myself, he was already walking away down the platform towards the exit. At the top of the stairs he paused to wave, his back still facing me and his head turned away, as if he was taking his final leave from the stage at the end of a performance. And then he vanished.

I opened his present as soon as my train pulled out of the station. It was a handsome hardcover edition of stories by Akutagawa, translated into English. Inside, Stanley had written a note directing me to read 'The Spider Thread'. It isn't a long story, just a few pages. I recalled that Stanley had crammed it into three sheets of a rough exercise book. I finished it quickly, put the book away and watched the darkness spread like a stain over the towns and villages on the outskirts of the city. I was disappointed that Stanley hadn't written me a letter or enclosed something more personal with his gift, and then I remembered how typical it was for him to frustrate my expectations in this way, to tease me with gestures that were intimate and impersonal at the same time. It was only hours later, in the middle of the night that I understood why the story had such a hold over him. It is about a career thief who goes to hell for his sins, then is offered a lifeline by the Buddha, a chance to atone. What happens and how is not as important as the story's theme, which is compassion. The thief has none. He is out for himself. At the end of the story, the Buddha breaks the thread and the thief tumbles back down into the river of blood to join all the other sinners. I have read the story many times since then and am always confused by it, mainly because my sympathies tend to be with the thief and never with the Buddha.

25

I didn't hear from Stanley for some months after my visit to Japan, even though I wrote to thank him for the book and for seeing me to my train. And then I received the first of a series of New Year cards from him that all said the same thing. *To dear Arthur, Happy New Year from your good friend Saburo*. I still have five of them, four earlier ones posted from Nagasaki and a later one postmarked New York. This last one also contained a photograph of Stanley taken on a New York street—he is surrounded by young American sailors, about six or seven of them, all wearing their crisp white sailor suits and all smiling broadly for the camera. Stanley has his arms around the two in the middle and he is also smiling. On the back of the picture is a note from him which reads *I'm dreaming of a white Christmas!* After that I received no more cards.

I continued to write Stanley the occasional letter, telling him about my work and my son, inviting him to visit me in Brisbane. *You will always be welcome,* I wrote. It was my habit to sign these letters *with love.* Not that I imagine Stanley ever took much notice. I never even knew if he received my letters or read them, because he never replied. To be honest, I didn't really mind. The real reason I wrote to him and signed the letters the way I did is because for the few moments it took to compose them I could give myself up to longings that I knew to be futile and self-defeating. I was so unused to this sweet sensation that it never failed to take me by surprise. And then I'd remember how I first came upon it.

Sometimes I drove up to Tatura from Melbourne if I was in town visiting Stuart. Of course there was nothing left of the camp by that time, and no obvious sign that it had ever been there. Apart from a few ruined walls and rolls of wire, the whole place had reverted to paddock. On my last visit I took some pictures of the countryside around where I estimated the infirmary had stood, and of the concrete foundations, which are all that remained of the kitchens. I also took a photograph of the hillside where I calculated the graveyard must have been, and where I imagined Baba-san had been buried. I sat for a while on the grass where the back steps of the infirmary had been and stared out at the scene. Without the perimeter fence interrupting the view, it was very different, of course, but the hills were unchanged, and the same sheep followed each other in single file through the same long grass.

I took the photographs with me when I visited Matron Conlon before she died in 1977. She was in a nursing home by then, unable to remember the day of the week. But she remembered me. As soon as I came into view she smiled and tried to sit up in her bed.

'Why aren't you in uniform?' she said.

'I left the army.'

'So you did. You found a girl.'

The photographs unfortunately meant nothing to her. She stared at them for a long time, then handed them back to me. 'I think it was a terrible mistake,' she said.

I asked her what she meant but she simply gazed at me out of her watery eyes and shook her head as if she was sworn to secrecy.

26

A short time after Matron Conlon's death, I received an invitation from McMaster to attend a gathering organised in Sydney. A former internee by the name of Kobayashi and his wife were now living in North Ryde, he wrote, with their eldest son Stephen.

Kobayashi was in Hay during the war so you wouldn't remember him, but you might remember the wife. She was one of the group from the Dutch East Indies, half-Indonesian, half-Japanese.

According to McMaster the couple had managed to send Stephen to Australia to study before they themselves had finally settled here.

I wrote back that I'd be very pleased to attend, but as the time approached for me to make arrangements to travel down to Sydney, I became less and less inclined to go and in the end I called McMaster to apologise for my absence, citing work commitments. He made me promise to keep in touch. He was writing a book, he said, based on his wartime diaries. He might want to talk to me at some stage about what I remembered.

'Now that we're all losing our faculties,' he said, 'I think it's important to write this stuff down.'

'Of course,' I said. 'Whenever you're in Brisbane.'

The next week he was at my door, briefcase in hand, a wild look in his eye that told me he had no time to waste. Now in his late seventies, McMaster was smaller than I remembered, and completely white-haired. I was moved to see him. I think I regarded him as my one remaining link with the war, the only living soul I knew, apart from May, who had any inkling about my life at Tatura or about the events of that time as they related to me.

I made us some coffee and took him out onto the back verandah where the winter sun warms that side of the house. We sat across from each other with all his papers spread out on the table in front of us.

'You missed a good lunch,' he told me. 'There were quite a few turned up that I thought I'd never see again.'

He reeled off a few names that I remembered from the school roll, even if I couldn't immediately picture the faces that went with them. All except for Sophie, whom I instantly recalled, particularly my last glimpse of her retreating down the corridor of the infirmary with her arms swinging and the huge weight of her belly threatening to overbalance her.

'Wonder of wonders,' said McMaster, 'if she doesn't show up with Bryant. Married to him for thirty-something years. Six kids.'

I said nothing. He fished out an old photograph, a gift from Bryant, and pushed it across the table to me. It showed the happy couple with their children lined up beside them, all plump and smiling, like a football team.

'He came back for her after she gave birth at the camp,' said McMaster. 'Married her to keep her from getting deported.'

I stared at the photograph for a long time then handed it back, while at the same time a great groundswell of indignation rose up inside me, a fit of pique at the injustice in allowing someone like Bryant any measure of satisfaction at all.

'He asked after you,' said McMaster. 'He said he had a theory about you.' He smiled at me and slipped the photograph back into its file.

'Are you going to tell me what it was?'

'He said he thought you had a secret life at Tatura that nobody knew anything about.'

Now it was my turn to smile.

'Did you?' he said.

'If I told you, I'd have to kill you,' I said.

McMaster laughed and sipped his coffee. He gazed out at the garden where the sun was making everything silvery.

'I must say I was surprised to see you at the docks that day. I never figured out what you were trying to prove.'

'Neither did I,' I said. 'But it was probably my finest hour.'

McMaster stayed for a couple of hours telling me all about his correspondence with former internees and guards. And then he asked me a question that I still find hard to answer.

'Do you think what the government did to the internees at Tatura was wrong? I mean morally.'

'I'm probably the wrong person to ask. Morality was never my strong suit.'

McMaster chortled in his deep-throated way. Apparently Bryant had said something similar when McMaster had asked him the same question. And then Bryant had gathered one of his pretty daughters up into his arms and told McMaster that it couldn't have been all bad if something as lovely as this had been the result.

After McMaster left that day I remained on the verandah lost in a fog of self-pity. It seemed to me that Bryant had somehow succeeded where I had failed, that he had exercised some superior will or had demonstrated some extra audacity, and that as a result he had walked away with the prize.

I must have stayed there for hours; by the time I finally came out of my reverie it was evening and a chill had descended over the garden. It was the time of year when the temperature plunges as soon as the sun goes down and my limbs had stiffened in the cooling air. I caught sight of myself in the glass of the kitchen window and saw an old man, hunched over and pale in the cold light, a dry husk where there had once been firm flesh and blood.

It struck me at that moment that May had been right to insist the war had taken some incalculable toll on me. And not only the war but also the secret life to which Bryant had referred, the burden of which I'd carried alone for so many years. I wanted to talk to May straight away, I wanted to tell her why I'd left her so suddenly that day and how I wasn't in my right mind then, and never had been. But by the time I found my way through the gloomy house to the telephone, my nerve had faltered. Instead I went to the kitchen and poured myself a fortifying mugful of whisky, then stood at the window nursing it while the darkness descended.

By about my fourth drink I had plucked up enough courage to sit down at my desk and write the letter to Stuart that I'd known for some time I owed him. In it I told him more or less coherently that I'd hidden my sexuality all my life in the mistaken belief that no other course of action was available to me. *I now see,* I wrote, *that this was not proof of my strength as I used to think, but a sign of weakness.* I then wrote four or five action-packed pages describing the events that had taken place in Tatura and afterwards, so that he would know the truth. At the end of the letter I wrote that my intention was not to hurt him with this new information. *On the contrary,* I said, *I hope you will see this as a belated gesture of the love I feel for you. Yours sincerely, Dad.*

When I finished writing I folded the pages away in an envelope and sealed it. On the front I wrote Stuart's name, then I filed the envelope with my birth certificate and my will in a manila folder I keep in the top drawer of my desk. The folder is marked *Official* and I've explained to Stuart what it contains in case he ever needs to find my papers in a hurry.

I would like to be able to tell you that this is where the letter remained. However, within a week I'd already moved it twice—the first time to a lower drawer in which I keep my photographs of Stanley and his postcards, along with old tax returns and certificates for shares I no longer own—the second time to my bookcase where I slipped it between the pages of a faded paperback history of Japan that I bought on my trip to see Stanley in 1963. About a month after that, in another whisky-fuelled fit of inspiration, I took the letter and the book down from the bookcase and burned them both outside in a bucket until they were reduced to ashes. I had by then decided that only a coward would write such a letter to his son and that the honest thing to do would be to tell my story to his face at a time when I judged he was ready to hear it. Which of course I prayed may be never.

As I doused the smoking ashes with water from the garden hose and threw the whole mess onto the hibiscus bushes at the back of the kitchen I told myself that this was an end to it. I vowed to disallow visions of Stanley before they had a chance to take hold in my head, to give him no conscious thought or speculation. In this way, I decided, I would free myself from the memory of that time, in the manner of a cure. And I'm pleased to report that, for a couple of years, I was reasonably successful. I conducted myself much as a recovering alcoholic might, counting the days off one by one. I threw myself into new hobbies: social tennis and golf, volunteering at the local soup kitchen, where every single man I laid eyes on reminded me of my father.

Nevertheless, I continued to feel, as many people do, that my real life had somehow evaded me, branched off at a crucial juncture and carried on without me in a more rewarding direction. I didn't need any proof that I'd missed out on something better than I had, but it came anyway, completely unannounced and, to my mind, unassailable. I arrived home from work one summer evening in 1981 to find a parcel on my front doorstep wrapped in brown paper and postmarked Nagasaki. Inside the parcel I discovered Stanley's suitcase, the old one from the camp, containing all of his books and travel souvenirs. Stuck on the outside of the suitcase was a sheet of yellowing paper on which Stanley had written my name and address and a note: *If I die please send to the above.*

The parcel also contained a letter, not from Stanley, but from a certain William Lewisham. He had thoughtfully enclosed a photograph of himself at Stanley's side. The two of them were posed in front of a restaurant called *Huck Finn's*. William, a tall rangy blond, had his finger pointing to a sign above the doorway that read *Nagasaki, Japan. Est. 1978.* His letter was friendly, almost intimate.

It's so fucking inconceivable. I kissed him goodbye when he left for his walk and that was the last time I saw him alive. The only good thing is that it was quick. The woman who found him told me that her dog started howling so she came out of her house and found Stanley on his knees in the street. The next thing his heart stopped. It's like a light has gone out and left the rest of us to stumble around in the dark. He's buried up on a hillside looking over the city because I can't bear to think of him anywhere that doesn't have a view. Yours in sorrow, Will.

For days I left the suitcase untouched. I was unable to decide whether to simply close it up and store it in a cupboard, or sort through its contents. Finally I took Stanley's books and placed

270

them on a bookshelf in my living room, and the rest I bundled together in an envelope, intending to send copies to McMaster in case he could use them in his memoir. I placed the suitcase itself underneath a side table inside my front door. It comforted me to see it there every time I came home, likewise the books. I never looked at their pages without remembering how Stanley had read aloud to me in the infirmary. I hadn't understood his Japanese then, and the script remained incomprehensible to me now, a secret code that I would never crack.

This didn't stop me trying. I would stare at a single character and will its meaning to come to me. When that failed I would move my eye to the next character and the next one after that. I even invested in a character dictionary and began to copy the characters one by one into an exercise book. I didn't imagine I would learn the language by this method, but it was a soothing pastime, one I still practise on a regular basis in order to calm my nerves.

If I failed to banish Stanley from my waking thoughts, I was even less successful at eradicating him from my dreams. He would show up uninvited while I was sleeping, mostly in all the old familiar places. He would be outside the Tatura schoolroom wearing his tennis whites, or standing on the parade ground in his funeral suit and charity shoes. Sometimes he was an older man trotting along a railway-station platform, waving to my departing train and trying at the same time to tell me something through the inch-thick glass that separated us.

The dream that I found hardest to wake from, and still do to this day, is the one where he is standing in the doorway of the infirmary at Tatura holding onto his suitcase and smiling straight at me. I always experience this smile in the same way, as emitting a sort of radiant warmth that I feel on the inside rather than on the surface of my skin. And then it is as if hot tears are welling up behind my eyes, although I have no way of knowing whether they are tears of gratitude or tears of grief.

While I wouldn't claim to know the meaning of the dream I am certain of one thing, which is that over time this spectre of Stanley has lost none of its power to rouse in me the most unreasonable feeling of joy. I'm persuaded for a moment that Stanley is in the room and that the next thing I will hear will be the sound of his miraculous voice. If I wake at that point in the dream, which I invariably do, it is with jubilation, as if in the course of the night some long-awaited reversal of fortune had restored to me everything that I've lost.

Acknowledgments

I am indebted to: Barbara Masel, Benjamin Law, Krissy Kneen, Caro Cooper and the extraordinary Penny Hueston.

This book would not have been possible without Yuriko Nagata who did all the groundwork and was constantly on hand to take my questions.

Many thanks to the Australia Council for their financial support during the writing of this book.

And thanks to my family as ever.